Different Sides to the Game: True Love Never Dies

Part 2

Ivana White-Drummond

You can put my books on your dresser now♡ I love you so much Lots of Love & Light sending your way. Congrats♡

Previously

I was working when my dad told me to come to DR ASAP. I didn't have the slightest clue as in why he was in a sudden rush for me to get there. I talked to him a few times since we first met, and I knew he and my mom called themselves sparking that old flame. But I still wasn't fully there yet to talk to him. When I got home, I had Reds' fat ass with me because he said she was the only one I could bring. I was in the middle of packing a bag when True came walking into my room with a concerned look.

"Where are you going?" he asked, walking over to me, taking my shirt out my hand. He actually looked afraid.

"To DR. I think something is wrong with my mom, so I'm just going to check it out. Don't worry, I'm not leaving you. But I do need you to watch Meen. Pleaseeeeee..." I begged, making him chuckle before he kissed my lips.

"Yeah, I'll watch him, shouldn't have to ask. Let me know how it goes though. Hit me as soon as you touch down. Take the jet," he said. True was so good to me, and I was starting to love him something terrible.

"You know I love you, right?" I let slip out my mouth. His eyes got big, making me nervous, before he smirked, pulling me into him. He kissed me passionately then pulled away.

"I love you too, gray eyes." He smiled, kissing me again. When he walked out the room, Kiera started calling my phone. Amber sucked her teeth before I answered.

"What's up?" I said, placing her on speaker.

"I thought we were friends!" Kiera yelled into the phone.

"What do you want, Kiera?" I said while Reds rolled her eyes.

"How is my best friend putting someone on my man!" she yelled.

"Who your man? 'Cause last time I checked, you cheated on him, and last time I checked, you wasn't my best friend," I snapped into the phone.

"Did you put them together, Lee?" She sniffed in the phone. 'The bitch has feelings,' I mouthed to Reds, making her chuckle.

"No. I didn't, Kiera. That was their choice."

"Whatever! You were always jealous of me!" she yelled.

"Girl, save that jealousy shit for a bitch who actually wants your life. Bye," I said, hanging up.

"She's so delusional," Amber said, making me laugh. We hadn't really spoken to Kiera for a while. She'd been rubbing us the wrong way, so we fell back. Then she just stopped showing up to work. I figured since her and Rico broke up, she lost it all or whatever. Rico even said she became a little stalker, which fit her perfectly. Of course. But it was what it was. She'd been on some shady shit, and I wasn't feeling it at all.

Within the next hour, we were up in the air, on our way to Dominican Republic. I couldn't stop wondering what Dom wanted for him not to want True or Mack to come. Four hours later, we landed in Punta Cana, Dominican Republic. A car was there waiting for us and took us to Dom's palace.

"Girl, I love your dad's house. I needs me one of those!" Amber said, looking up at Dom's home. Getting out the car, my mom opened the house door with a strange look on her face.

"What's up, Mom? Why Dad wanted us to come here?" I asked, giving her a hug. She kissed my cheek and smiled, and a tear slipped out of her eye.

"Mom, what's wrong?" We said in unison.

"I'm just happy, damn." She sucked her teeth, making us laugh. "But your dad is in his office. Go talk to him," she said before walking away. As we walked toward my dad's office, something felt weird. I felt him. I felt his presence. All these years, I'd never felt his energy this heavy. I stopped walking, feeling my heart start to beat fast. Amber looked back at me, confused. Maybe I was tripping. There was no way I could feel him. I was tripping… had to be.

Opening the door, my dad was talking to some guy; his back was facing the door. He looked up at me, giving me a faint smile, then looked at the guy who turned around. I thought my mind was playing tricks on me. My heart instantly *fell to my stomach. I smelled him, I felt him, our energy was always that strong. Looking over at Amber to make sure she was seeing what I was seeing, she had tears flowing down her face. So maybe I'm not tripping.*

   "Ahmeen?"

Saaleha Santana

Unexpected Visitor

"Ahmeen?" I said softly, I couldn't believe I was face to face with my husband. His skin tone was tanned due to the Dominican Republic weather. His body was filled with muscles, and his sunni beard was perfect. He still looked the same. I couldn't believe my eyes. I stood there in complete shock. Confused. All these years went by, and he was still alive. It couldn't be. I saw his body with my own two eyes. He was dead. He started toward me, and I backed up. This couldn't be real. He opened and closed his mouth while nothing came out, before his eyes went to Amber who had tears flowing down her face. After all this time, he was alive, right here in the flesh. My heart rate started to speed up before the tears finally fell. I spun around on my heels, abruptly running out the room.

"Saaleha!" I heard him yell behind me, but I didn't stop walking. How could he do this to me, to his son, to his family? Tears clouded my vision as I walked through my father's estate with no clue of where I was going. "Baby, wait. Pocahontas, listen to me!"

Feeling him touch me instantly made me stop walking. I turned around with my chest heaving up and down, staring at him. He really faked his death and wanted me to listen to him, listen to what he had to say. He had five years to talk, five years to explain. So many thoughts were running through my head at this moment. He left me! He left my son! He went to grab me again, but this time I was quicker and punched him dead in the face, instantly drawing blood from his lip and nose. He stepped back, wiping the blood before chuckling.

"Don't fucking touch me! Five years, Ahmeen! Five damn years?" I screamed, hitting him again harder, crying harder. He pulled me into him, but I didn't stop fighting him. "How could you do that to me! How could you do that to Lil' Meen! My son suffered without his father! Why would you do this!" I felt my body shaking as I backed away from him, staring at him. All I kept thinking was that he really was alive.

"Baby, you need to listen to him. Let him explain," my mom said, causing my head to snap in her direction. Was she serious? Amber looked at my mom in complete confusion. *What did she mean listen to him? Did she know?*, I thought to myself.

"No! Nobody gets to tell me to calm down! Nobody! You knew, Mom? Y'all knew this nigga was still alive, but y'all allowed me to be miserable for all these years! Crying and begging God to send you back to me, and the whole time you were still alive!" I screamed.

"Can you please listen, Pocahontas?" Ahmeen said softly. I snapped my head back in his direction before shaking my head.

"Fuck you, Ahmeen." I stormed off, and he ran after me again, this time, yanking my arm and pulling me into a room. He slammed the door and pushed me against it. Ahmeen's hazel eyes stared into mine, causing me to break even more; he was really alive.

"How could you hurt me like that? Ahmeen, I waited up every single day, thinking maybe you weren't really dead. I had the dream. God was telling me you were still here. I felt it. But I believed my eyes. Damn... My own lies were lying to me. The fuck!" I yelled, pushing him away.

"It's complicated as fuck, Lee—"

"Well get to explaining! We're married. You just don't leave me in the dark. Tell me what the hell was so complicated that you had to fake your damn death and leave me and your kid out of your life? Momma was right! She said you weren't always going to love me! She was right!" I screamed, pushing him away, and this time he let go. Stepping back, his face balled up, and he stared at me as if he had the utmost disbelief. He had some nerve.

"What, Saaleha? I never stopped loving your fucking dumb ass! You my wife! I never fell out of love with you. I watched you every day. You think I didn't want to just come home? I couldn't, to protect my fucking family! Niggas wanted me dead! And it only took two mediocre ass bitches to put me down," Ahmeen yelled. His face was beet red. I didn't care about his nut ass attitude. "Don't say I don't love you! I did all this to protect you!" I reached out to touch his face. *I can't believe he was here, breathing,* I thought to myself.

"Ahmeen, I could kill you right now."

"You really think I didn't love you?" Ahmeen asked. Walking closer to me, I wanted to punch his stupid ass again, but his lip and nose was still bleeding. So that was good enough for me. *I got his ass good,* I thought before smirking lightly.

"You left me. I was angry! I thought you were selfish for dying on me. Now you just a selfish bitch that faked his death." I rolled my eyes, making him chuckle. I don't know what he thought was funny, I was literally boiling right now. He had me so messed up right now.

"There she goes. I was only able to get her to come out when you were mad." Ahmeen shook his head. I remember when we first met, I was so soft and sweet, but after years of being his girl, he would irk me to extreme measures! Which made me develop, what he referred to as a mean streak. I didn't care either, because he used to just antagonize me.

"The doctor? Did she work for you? Because she couldn't look me in my eyes that night; I remember. She wouldn't look at me when she came out, until she walked away. I never forgot about that, because it didn't sit right with me," I asked, remembering that doctor that night because when I went back to see her, they said she quit.

"Yeah. Your dad paid her to move to the DR and take care of me," Ahmeen said. I couldn't believe them, after all this damn time. I always knew something wasn't right. I should've gone with my gut, but damn it was hard because I saw him dead.

"You were dead," I said softly.

"Nah. I just looked dead. It was anesthesia, or some fly shit like that," his dumb ass said like this shit was normal. Like, how much time did he really have on his hands to do some bullshit like this. I just couldn't deal with this stuff. "I have a boyfriend now," I said instantly thinking of True. What am I going to do with True? How was he going to feel once I told him that Ahmeen was really alive? I had some many questions to ask myself, at this point my life was an official roller coaster with no brakes.

"Naw, you got a temporary placeholder. I'ma get my family back, if it's the last thing I do," he said so seriously. I just knew that what he was saying held so much weight because I knew him. I knew he would stop at nothing to get me back, but I knew I couldn't do that to True. Especially not after he lost his wife. I was so confused right now. I didn't know what to do.

Ahmeen Santana

The King is Back

It felt good to finally be back. I knew my family was going to be disappointed in me, but I had to do what I had to do for my family. Even though, I knew Saaleha doesn't understand now, I knew she would one day. I just had to do this for myself and to protect my wife and son. I didn't know how much people hated me because I was getting money, but when Rasta came to the hospital the night I was supposed to die and ran everything down to me, I wanted blood. Saaleha's dad, Dominick, who was my plug, told me to lay low and let them think they were winning. Rasta's nephew Ronnie put a hit out on me, even though nobody was stupid enough to go through with the hit. But Kiera and Omar were. Yeah, I knew exactly who *killed* me. After all these years, I was able to finally find Ronnie, and when a nigga's life was on the line, they'll talk. He talked until I pulled the trigger. My own wife's best friend. I always knew I couldn't trust that bitch for a reason! Then I felt mad disrespected because the hit was only fifty thousand dollars. If anybody was going to take me out, it needed to be over a couple mill. I was a valuable man.

"I swear I love y'all. Y'all better never give my shit away," I heard Ronnie *groan after he just got finish having sex with my cousin Kim and her girlfriend Nikki. "Y'all hear me!" he barked, but the only thing the girls did was smirk when they saw me walking up.*

"Yeah, nigga, they heard you." I chuckled with my AK 47 pointed at the back of Ronnie's head.

"Y'all bitches set me up!" Ronnie snapped, making them laugh.

"You shouldn't have tried to kill my cousin, nigga. Fuck you," Kim spat, leaving him confused until I walked around the sofa, and his eyes lit up.

"See, you sent that little weak bitch Kiera to do some shit she had no business doing." Kim chuckled as she continued to put her clothes on.

"You too, Nikki?" Ronnie said in disbelief.

"Nigga, yeah. Kim is my whole ass girlfriend. Couldn't you tell?" She chuckled before grabbing Kim's butt.

"Everybody knew Kim was my cousin, bro, and everybody knew Kim loved herself some pussy. Nikki's to be exact." I shook my head. About a year ago, I sent for my cousin Kim to come out to the Dominican Republic so we could come up with this plan. After she cursed me out for lying about my death, we came up with the plan where Kim and Nikki would seduce Ronnie and make their way into his life, which was easy for those two because they were the most wanted strippers coming out of Vanity Grand.

"So where were you for all those years then, nigga? Why you just coming for me?" Ronnie yelled. He wanted to play tough, but I knew he was ready to piss himself.

"Living life, chilling. Letting you build yourself up just so I can kill you, bro. Funny thing is, your uncle knew I was alive too. And he's another reason why I'm here and shit." Shaking my head, I cocked my gun back.

"Come on, man. I'm sorry. I was a kid. I made a mistake," Ronnie cried out. He was scared as hell. Punk ass, I thought while smirking.

"I told those niggas you were some weak ass gangsta. Nigga, die with some dignity." Kim shook her head before grabbing Nikki's hand and walking out of the living room, before yelling out, "Oh, Meen, you owe me so much money for fucking his ugly ass."

"Kiera wanted to do that shit, man. She hated Saaleha, and she wanted to make her suffer. She even hated Amber, man. Some shit about when she was a kid, and she wanted them to suffer. Bro, I'm telling you this shit was her idea. She came to me! I was hating, no lie, bro. So, I ordered that little ass hit, knowing nobody was going to take the bait, but on my momma, this was all Kiera's idea," Ronnie pleaded, making me lower my gun. Kiera foul, I shook my head.

"Damn, that bitch been grimy, huh? I always told Saaleha." I chuckled, noticing Ronnie getting relaxed, just how I wanted him.

"Yeah, man. She also said Saaleha took you from her. She said she saw you first and called dibs or some shit like that. Bro, the bitch got it bad for them. She hates them so bad, she even said she tried to fuck Mack, but he wasn't with that shit. Even after you died, she tried to ruin their lives some type of way," Ronnie *spoke confidently. Looking up at him, I shook my head. Niggas really do fold under pressure. "Thanks for not killing me, bro. We can go after Kiera together if you want."*

"Naw, I don't need no weak niggas on my team. Thanks for the information though," was all I said before letting two shots into Ronnie's head. *"Bitch ass nigga."* I chuckled before picking up the phone and calling Jay.

"Yo bro," Jay answered after the first ring.

"I dropped all this wine on the fucking carpet, bro. Can you call that company for me? It's a dud." Speaking in code, I requested a cleanup crew.

"Clumsy ass nigga, man. I got you," Jay replied before hanging up the phone. I looked at Ronnie one more time. A part of me believed everything he said, that it wasn't his fault. Rasta even said he was too weak of a nigga to pull something like that off, but what's done is done.

Kiera was next.

I just hated that I had to do that to Saaleha, let alone my son, but I had to protect them. I knew it would've killed Saaleha when I finally came back, but she'll get over it sooner than later. Hopefully. Something was up with Kiera, and if she was willing to hurt Saaleha anyway she could, I knew she wasn't finish. When True came around, it pissed me off because he knew she was my wife. I knew I was being selfish, but that nigga shouldn't have moved in on my wife like that, especially when he was still married. I knew about his wife dying too. Monica was cool back then, anytime I was in New York for business. Now, he was the reason why my own wife wouldn't talk to me. Well, I mean I know I played a huge part in it too, for faking my death and all; but still. I hadn't really spoken with Saaleha since she left. She hadn't been returning any of my calls.

"I wish you stop freaking calling me!" she yelled when she answered the phone. I smiled picturing her pretty ass face balled up. I took a deep breath, while she did the same. We stayed silent for about a minute, before her soft voice flowed through the phone again.

"You have to give me time. I know you want to see him, but you have to give me time."

"How long, Pocahontas?" I sucked my teeth, instantly knowing that was the wrong move just by the sucking of her teeth.

"However long I say, boy. You wouldn't have to be asking to see him if you never faked your damn death. Dickhead!" she screamed out, making me chuckle. I knew I was going to have a whole lot of ass kissing to do with her stubborn ass.

"Well, when you coming to see me?"

"Nigga, I have a man. Ain't nobody coming to see you." She sucked her teeth, fronting like she didn't still love a nigga. I knew what I did was fucked up, but I also knew Saaleha loved my dirty drawers. She could front all she wanted.

"And you have a husband."

"Goodbye, Ahmeen Santana. I'll let you know when you can see him," she said, not giving me a chance to respond, because she hung up on me. Damn, I'm going to have to do a lot of ass kissing, but damn, I thought she would've been happier to see me. Then, she keeps talking this she got a man shit, as if I cared. I was still her husband, and she was going to get back on board because it was 'til death do us part. And last time I checked, neither one of us was dead.

"'Bout time y'all niggas got here." I smiled, opening the door for Mack and Jay. They both were out here looking like pretty boys, probably because of Saaleha and Reds, keeping them in check. Jay looked at me before sucking his teeth, forcing a laugh out of me.

"Nigga, 'bout time you decided to tell Saaleha you not really dead," Jay snapped before pushing past me in the door. Chuckling, I looked over at Mack who was shaking his head. I went to give him a handshake, but he knocked my hand out his way and walked in the house.

"Nah, I've been getting questioned by Amber overly hyped ass as if she was the FEDs. No matter how many times I lie and say I didn't know, she just knows I knew. Her ass be reading me, I swear," Mack stated, making Jay and I laugh. Reds always knew when he was lying; he would always get caught with shit.

Yes. My brothers knew about me faking my death. At first, they didn't know because I needed to know who was trying to take me out. Saaleha's dad, Dom, told me it was somebody close to us, so I couldn't count out anyone. After six months of me being *dead*, I reached out to them. Of course, at first, they were pissed off with me. I even had to square up with them, one on one. But eventually, they got over it. They were there with me when I killed Ronnie because Jay was the one who found him. The hardest part of it all was hiding it from Saaleha.

"I should be the one mad at you, gon' allow True to talk to Lee." I sucked my teeth, while Mack shrugged his shoulders and Jay laughed.

"Papi," my chick of three years said as she walked into the living area of the house. Jay and Mack's head snapped in the direction of her, before they looked at me, shaking their heads. I tugged on my beard before chuckling. *Why did she have to bring her dippy ass down here*, I thought to myself. "Oh, I didn't know you had company. I'm Kristina."

Kris's and I relationship was just as complicated as my life. She was originally from Mexico, but she stayed in Miami now, handling her father's business. I met her through her dad, Jose. He said he always wanted a son but got blessed with a daughter. So, she had no choice on taking over her father's empire, with the help of me of course. Her body was out of this world, that she got done on my dime, and I loved how she switched up her hairstyles. She reminded me G Herbo's baby mom, Ari. I'm not going to sit here and front like I didn't appreciate Kris, but she wasn't Saaleha. And knowing that I was still married to Lee, restricted me to a lot of things with Kristina. I did my thing, she did her thing, and majority of the time, we did us.

"Can we talk for a second, babe?" was all she said before she walked out of the living room, not even giving me a chance to say a word. I looked over at Mack and Jay, who both wore a smug grin before they laughed.

"And I'm glad my sis found a new nigga. Look at you, living it up with fake ass JLO," Mack finally returned, making Jay and I fall out laughing. This nigga was stupid.

Shaking my head, I got up and headed to my bedroom because I knew that's where she went. When I got to the bedroom, Kristina's high yellow skin tone was beet red. She was standing in the middle of the bedroom with her hand on her hips and her head cocked to the side.

"What's your problem?" I inquired before taking a seat on the chair that was in the bedroom. Leaning back, I kicked my feet up on the ottoman and crossed my arms, watching her sexy ass pout.

"My problem? Ahmeen, you said you was going to give me time before you decided to tell your so-called wife about you being alive. We had a deal!" She spoke very angrily before she walked over and stood in front of me.

"I gave you ample time, Kris. I told you the day was coming soon. Plus, I got you your father's empire. I helped you tremendously. So technically, babe, I handled my part of the deal." I licked my lips before looking her up and down.

"Where does that leave us, Meen? I love you. You can't just push me to the side. She doesn't even know you how I know you. She knows the old you. What can a fucking hairstylist do for you? I help you run this drug business! What can she do? Shape you up?" she yelled, forcing her accent to come out. Here she goes, making my dick hard. I thought while biting my lip looking at her.

"She's my wife, Kristina. That's where it leaves us. I'm married to her, whether she's a hairstylist or into running a drug empire like I used to. She's still my wife, and when I married her, I vowed death do us part. I'm not dead, and neither is she." Simply shrugging, I stood up, fixing my erection, which caused Kris's eyes to fly to it and smirk a little. "I don't want to hear nothing about Saaleha; that's my wife. Remain in your lane, until otherwise."

"What do y'all see in this bitch?" she whispered under her breath, but I heard her. I didn't know what that meant, but I wasn't wasting time on figuring it out. I didn't have time for Kristina being in her feelings over shit she knew would happen. I had bigger and better fish to fry. I was back, and it was time to make my return known.

Kiera Mitchell

Night Terrors

"Why are you doing this, Lamont?" I stood in the corner of my bedroom while my stepbrother blocked me in. I was visiting my father, Kenny, in New York, and I wished I was home in Philly.

"You don't trust me, lil' sis?" Lamont asked before a soft smile graced his face, and he walked closer to me. I stood in the corner with a pair of Juicy Couture shorts on and a tank top. Even at fourteen, I had a nice body, after I hit puberty, of course. "Come on, I won't hurt you. Just come on."

Lamont spun on his heels, while grabbing my arm, basically dragging me with him. Our parents were out having a date night, so it was just me and Lamont in the house. I had never wished my dad was around so bad until now. We walked through the home until we got down to the basement where we were greeted by two of Lamont's friends. I stopped in my tracks, making Lamont turn to face me.

"You trust me?" was all he asked before his two friends walked toward me. I tried to back away, but Lamont grabbed my hair, forcing me to stay in position.

"Please, no! Lamont! Please, no!"

"Kee! Yo, wake up, ma!" I felt Omar tapping me, forcing me out of my sleep. He pulled the covers back as I laid in a pool of my own sweat. I jumped up and leaned against the headboard, hugging my legs, rocking back and forth. Omar stared at me as if he was trying to figure out his next move. I hated to have those dreams, but they were a part of me.

I watched Omar as he walked out of his bedroom and came back with fresh sheets in his hand. Then he walked into the bathroom, cutting the shower water on. When he came back out, he set the sheets on the bed before he held his hand out for me. Grabbing his hand, he walked me into the bathroom, stripping me out of my clothes and helped me into the shower.

"Shower while I change the sheets. I can make you something quick to eat. I mean, it's about—" He paused before looking at the clock in the bathroom. "About 3:30 a.m. Is that cool with you?"

Nodding my head yes, he left out the bathroom, leaving me in my own thoughts. It was nothing I could do to stop those nightmares. I tried therapy, but it never helped. Or maybe it was because I stopped going to my therapy sessions. I always thought she was talking bullshit. I never really shared my life story with anyone, not even Saaleha and Amber. I wished I did though because I swear it played a huge part in my resentment toward them. Picking up the rag, I scrubbed my body, just remembering the worst summer of my life. I cried for the fourteen-year-old me. I cried for what I had to endure at that young age, before I finally got out. I stood in front of the bathroom mirror and was completely satisfied for who had I become. I came a long way, and I swear everybody was going to pay for what I went through, even if they weren't around.

Walking out the bathroom, I noticed the sheets were changed, and Omar had a sandwich out on the bed for me. I walked over to my overnight bag, pulling out a pair of shorts and a tank top. Slipping it on, I walked over to the bed and climbed in. I stayed quiet and so did Omar. After Cherelle gave birth to their son, he took the baby from her and moved out to Delaware. Lately, we'd been kicking it heavily. He'd been pressing me about a relationship. And even though I didn't have anyone else, I wasn't giving up on Rico that easily, especially after he called himself dating Aminah. I still couldn't believe Saaleha put them together. *Shady ass*, I thought.

Omar's and I situation was what it was. We'd link up every month for about a week or two and just spend it with each other. No questions asked about who we'd been spending time with, even though I knew he'd only been wrapped in his son, it would just him running a check up on me, and us having spontaneous sex. I still loved Omar, deeply, and I didn't think I'd ever love any man as much as I did him, but I just wanted more than him. I needed the *plug*. I needed the life Saaleha's and Red's lives.

"So, you not going to tell me who Lamont is? And why you are having nightmares of him?" Omar inquired, interrupting my thoughts. I looked over at him, noticing the concerned face, causing me to let out a deep breath.

"It's nothing. I just—"

"Stop lying all the time, Kee, like for real," he snapped. I leaned my back against the headboard before sighing. "I've known you damn near your entire life. I have never seen you like that. I watched you for a little before I woke you up. You kept saying his name and telling him no and to stop. Talk to me, Kee." He was so sincere. He cared. Even when I didn't want him to care, he did.

"He ruined my life, but that's all I'm willing to say right now," I said softly before grabbing his hand. He looked up at me before he leaned in to kiss me softly.

"Stop hiding from people that truly love you, Kee." He spoke so firmly. I wished I could've been open and honest with him. He had my back for years; I'd do anything for him just as he'd do anything for me. Omar was the perfect combination of lover and best friend for me. We just wasn't the perfect match.

"One day," was all I said before I climbed on top of him. I didn't want to talk about it, so me being me, I blocked it out with sex. I'd tell my truth one day, but today wasn't that day. I hated to be judged, and I knew that was what he was going to do. Judge me. Same as perfect little Reds and Lee.

True Taylor
I Got Your Back

♡

Ever since Saaleha came back from visiting her dad in Dominican Republic, she'd been acting mad weird. I mean, I couldn't really explain it, but she'd been clingy as fuck. We all knew she was anything but clingy, but she'd been around me a lot. Lil' Meen was coming home in like two weeks, from his basketball tournament he had left for as soon as Lee got back. So, I would think she'd be getting ready for him 'cause I knew she missed him. Then, on top of her being clingy, her ass has been mean as fuck, snapping on me then crying and shit. My chick had never been this bipolar. At first, I was thinking she was still mad about me not telling her about Monica, but she claimed she was over that. Her ass been tripping out, and every time I ask her what happened in DR, she just said nothing. I was going to find out though, sooner or later.

"Miss! You cannot go in there, he's busy!" I heard my assistant Megan yell, before my office door swung open and Saaleha's crazy ass walked in.

"I'm his woman. He's not that damn busy." Saaleha sucked her teeth, while placing her bag on the chair and walking over to my desk. Shaking my head at her newly psycho ass, I chuckled.

"Megan, she's fine," was all I said, but Megan's eyes held fear in them before she nodded and left out the room. Looking over to Saaleha, she wore a smug grin, causing me to shake my head. "Why are you here? And why are you bullying my workers?"

"Nobody was bullying her ass. She should've just let me come up." She rolled her eyes before sitting in front on my desk. We stared at each other for a little before she looked down at her hands.

"What's up, baby? Why you here?"

"I can't come see my *man* now? I missed you." Her smart ass pouted, rolling her neck and shit. Why her little ass gotta be rude, I thought while staring at my beautiful girlfriend. It was crazy to me being in a relationship with someone besides Monica, but I loved Lee.

"Lee, you came all the way to New York to see *your man*, when you know I'm coming home to you." Cocking my head to the side, I watched her bite her bottom lip like she was thinking, before she chuckled. Looking at me, she laughed a little harder before shrugging her shoulders. "'Cause you a spoiled brat; come here."

Getting up as she was told, she walked over to me and sat on my lap. "I really missed you." She smiled before kissing me softly, which was short lived because Montez came walking into my office. Saaleha sucked her teeth, forcing a laugh out of me, and Montez stuck his middle finger up at her.

"It's good to see you too, Lee," Tez said before taking a seat in front of my desk. Saaleha fake ass waved; they had a love/hate type relationship. "Where my girl at?"

"She's pregnant and in love, Tez. Let it go!" Saaleha said in reference to Reds.

"Man, fuck all that. Her pretty ass needs to fuck with me, for real. Mack cool and shit, but the way he be treating her is a dub." Montez was going hard. He'd been crushing on Amber for a while, but he wasn't the type to step on niggas' toes. Saaleha chuckled before shaking her head.

"You're annoying, I swear." Saaleha laughed before she faced me. "Tell him to leave. It's my time."

"He was mine before he was yours," Tez joked, making all of us laugh.

"That was so gay of you." Lee chuckled. "But for real, Tez. I want to spend time with my baby. You're interrupting."

Different Sides Of The Game 2

"Saaleha, you know I don't care about none of that shit," Tez spat before standing up. "But on a lighter note, when the next time you cooking?"

"Probably next week. Bye!" Lee leaned her head on my shoulder, while Tez put his middle finger up at her. We talked a little bit more before he headed out, leaving Lee and I alone. "I always wanted to do it on a desk." She smirked.

"Oh yeah?" Licking my lips, I placed her on the desk and ripped her panties off. She leaned back and pushed her denim skirt up more, showcasing her pretty pink lips. Her flower was so pretty to me, and it always smelled good. I licked my lips at the sight of her fingers slipping inside of flower while her eyes stayed on me. Biting my lip, I moved her hands and dove in head first.

"Baby," she moaned out as her hands flew to my head. Her hand ran through the man bun I was sporting. I sucked, licked, and nibbled as if it was about to be my last meal. "Fuck!" she screamed as she fucked my face back.

"Cum for me, Lee." I groaned into her flower. My eyes connected with hers, and it was the prettiest sight. Her mouth was wide open, her eyes held so much love in them, and her voice was caught in her throat. Licking her clit faster, that moan that was caught finally came out as a scream, all while she exploded inside of my mouth.

"I want you," she said so sexily, I felt my dick get harder than it already was. Unbuttoning my slacks, she slipped my dick out and guided it inside of her. Her mouth was ajar, and her head fell backwards. I had to sit there for a little, just to keep myself from cumming fast. "Please," she begged as she looked me in the eyes.

Biting my bottom lip, I stroked deeply inside of her, forcing her to grab onto me. Picking her legs up, I rammed inside of her while she wrapped her arms around my neck. I used that as my motivation to pick her up off the desk and slam her down onto me. The way she was feeling right now, man, her shit was so wet. Wetter than usual. I looked down, watching myself disappear inside of her, looking at her cum right onto my dick.

"Damn," I whispered, getting harder at the sight alone. Placing her back on the desk, I slipped out of her, instantly missing the feel of her. "Turn around," I demanded before I helped her climb off the desk. Bending Lee over the desk, I started to eat her out from the back.

"Trueeeeeee," she moaned out as she spread her ass open. I ran my tongue across her asshole before I came up. "Put it in." She demanded. Doing as I was told, I pushed Lee's body more onto the desk, arching her back deeper as I slid in and out of her.

"Fuck me back, baby. You know how I like it." I groaned before sticking my thumb in her butt. Which she used as motivation to throw it back onto me. My fingers gripped her sides, trying to keep my composure, but I knew I wouldn't last long. "Shit, Lee."

"Cum with me, daddy," she said as I pulled her body into mine, grabbing her neck. I turned her head to face me before kissing her passionately, allowing a little spit into her mouth because I knew she loved that shit. Her body jerked before she came onto my dick, and I exploded inside of her. Sliding out of her slowly, she dramatically fell forward, making me laugh.

"You're so extra." I chuckled before sitting back in my chair. She went into the bathroom that was in my office, before coming out with a rag in her hand. She cleaned the both of us up before she picked up her phone, which went off in the middle of us having sex. Her face balled up as she texted back, then another message came through.

"Babe, look at this." Saaleha turned her phone to face me so that I could read the messages.

Unknown: Your best friend Kiera isn't as innocent as she seems. She'll do anything to hurt you. She already caused you the worst pain ever.

Saaleha: Who is this?

Unknown: Watch your back.

"Let me see," was all I said before grabbing her phone. Picking up my phone, I sent the number to my tech guy so that he could track the phone. Once I finished, I handed her phone back to her. "When the last time you talked to her?"

"Um, the day I left for DR. She called me talking about I put Minah on Rico, and all this I was jealous of her bullshit." Saaleha shrugged her shoulders.

"Look, if she calls you or text you, just keep your distance like you been doing. I'm going to figure out who texted you that shit. Don't stress it." I paused just thinking about Kiera. "Wait, she used to pop pills?"

"Pills? Wrong bitch; Ki has never been on drugs. I would know; I've known her forever," Saaleha said, defending her.

"Didn't mean to offend you, babe. Maybe I do have the wrong person," I suggested, noticing her discomfort. I knew the truth. The niggas who used to work my block out here in New York used to sell to her. She started doing drugs with her stepbrother Lamont; that nigga actually got her hooked-on pills. I knew that she got that bull from South Philly, Omar hooked back on that shit too, but he went to coke while she stayed on pills. I was going to allow Saaleha to think what she wanted to think. I knew the truth. I'd be keeping an eye on Kiera and watching Saaleha's back.

Aminah Santana

New Lover &Things

After finding out my brother was still alive, I shut down. I couldn't believe he was that selfish that he faked his own death. My mom was all 'I needed to hear him out,' but I wasn't ready to. You just didn't do shit like that, so I'd been spending all my time with Rico. From him picking me up from school and work, I saw him almost every day or every other day. Everything about him was all around amazing. He'd been like a breath of fresh air. Being with him was different for me. I didn't know if it was because he was older; well, the first order guy I'd ever dealt with. He always took me out on dates, always purchased me things, even without me asking, and we'd cake on the phone all night. And he always wanted to spend time with me whenever he wasn't busy working. He was just perfect. Today, I was finally going to his home in North Jersey, and I was so nervous. He broke his lease at the Cherry Hill Towers because he said Kiera kept popping up at the building, causing a scene because she couldn't get in. I keep telling Rico that when I finally catch her, I'm beating up her up and it's nothing he can do to stop me, period.

"Who is this guy you've been spending a lot of time with?" my mom asked as she walked into my bedroom.

"He's a friend. His name Rico," I replied, slipping my Adidas track pants on.

"Can I meet him?" she asked. Turning around, I took my mom in. She hadn't aged a bit and honestly could pass as my sister with her blue eyes and long sandy brown hair. My mom was drop dead gorgeous and the strongest woman I knew. After my dad left us, she never let it affect her, it was like she took it on the chin and kept on. I admired her for that, she showed me that you actually don't need a man, that you can do it on your own. We'd always had a very close relationship, I mean how could we not it was always me, her, and Meen. Then just me and her. I cherished the ground my mother walked on.

"Yes, when I'm ready for you to meet him, Mommy."

"Okay, no rush, no rush. I just want to make sure you have a keeper," was all she said smiling, before she left out my room. I continued to get dressed, putting my hair up in a high ponytail. My phone went off with a text from Rico, saying he was outside. Grabbing my purse, I headed outside. When I got inside of Rico's Mercedes S550, he kissed me softly, bringing a smile out of me.

"I swear you switch cars like you switch drawers." I laughed, making him chuckle.

"I just like to change it up, you know?" He smirked. This man is just so fine sitting over there, I smirked just looking at him. He was sitting in the drivers' seat in dressed down, which was something he never does because he's always in suits. He wore a pair of black jeans and a Fendi t-shirt, his hair was freshly cut, and his cologne lit up the whole car.

"How was your day?" I asked while reclining my chair back, getting comfortable for this two-hour ride.

"Girl, it's only 4 p.m.; my day still going," he said, making me lean up and look at the clock on the dashboard then laugh.

"Oh shit. Swore it was later. Well, man, how was your day so far?"

"Pretty smile, pretty eyes," Rico said before looking back on the road, making butterflies form in my stomach. "But it was okay. Nothing big happened. I just had to tie up some loose ends." He shrugged. "What you do today?"

"Well, I told you I was going to go look at that dance studio that's downtown. I loved it, but I want you to go down there with me to look at it."

"You don't want your brother to go? You know since he's—"

"I'm still not talking to him," I interrupted him, rolling my eyes just thinking about Ahmeen's selfish ass. I knew I wasn't in the wrong either, because Saaleha was still ignoring him too.

"La Bella, you have to talk to him." Rico sighed before squeezing my hand. "But I'll go with you. Just promise me that you'll talk to him soon."

"Fine." I mumbled before looking out the window. For the rest of the ride, we just talked, and I gave him a little talent show, even though he laughed at me. But I knew he enjoyed it because I was the next Beyoncé, period. Eventually, I drifted off to sleep, before hearing Rico calling my name. Stirring a little in my sleep, I finally opened my eyes, and got damn was his house amazing. I mean so ah-maz-ing, I was ready to just move in. The home looked like something that belonged in Calabasas or some Beverly Hills type stuff.

"Got damn." I paused before looking at Rico. "This is so nice." Grabbing my things, I climbed out of his car and stared up at his home. "CoCo, this is soooo nice." I smiled. Looking back at him, I noticed his face was balled up. "What?"

"You really pretty, La Bella. But don't call me that CoCo shit. What I look like?" He sucked his teeth, walking past me. I chuckled because I really liked the name and it just came to me.

"How about only when we're alone? You'll get used to it. I like the name." I shrugged with a grin on my face. "CoCo is such a cute nickname."

"Minah, I'm not playing." He stared at me, forcing me to throw my hands up in a surrendering way and chuckle.

"Okay, mean ass. Fine." I chuckled while taking my shoes off by the door.

"Why you take your shoes off?"

"Sign of respect. And plus, it looks like you just got these nice marble floors waxed." I chuckled, walking around and touring the house while Rico headed upstairs to the shower. Once I finished my tour, I headed to the master bedroom where I heard the shower running. Letting my curiosity get the best of me, I walked into the bathroom, instantly seeing the reflection of Rico. Licking my lips, I walked over to the shower and opened it. He stared at me, while I watched the water bounce off his body. My eyes traveled down to his member, causing my mouth to drop. He was packing something serious. Looking up at his face, he wore a smug grin, like he just knew he was that nigga.

"You getting in? Or you just going to stand there letting the cold ass air in?" he asked, washing his face off. I stood there, debating with myself, before I walked away, making him laugh. Walking into the bedroom, I stood there racking my brain before I took my clothes off and laid on his bed. Spreading my legs apart, I slipped my fingers in between my treasure, and started pleasuring myself with thoughts of Rico in my head.

"You thinking about me?" His deep voice boomed throughout the room, scaring me half to death. Looking up, I started to move my hand before he spoke again. "Nah, don't stop." Walking over to me, he removed my finger and started rubbing his finger up and down my slit. "Damn," he groaned. We stared at each other as he leaned in to kiss me with so much passion, causing me to moan even louder inside his mouth. He pulled away and inserted his finger.

"Fuck," I moaned out, as his finger went deeper while stroking my clit with his thumb. He kept that movement going on until I grabbed his hand.

"Don't touch me," he said, and I instantly moved my hand. His piercing green eyes stared into my blue ones. I was so mesmerized by him. His member was so rock hard, but I couldn't take it there with him yet. It was too soon, in my opinion.

"Baby, I'm going to cum," I moaned out as I rode his fingers. Biting his bottom lip, he sped up his fingers before he removed them completely and latched onto my clit. "Rico!" I moaned out as I came harder than I ever came from head, into his mouth. Once I finished coming down off my high, I watched him take his fingers and rub around my flower, then stuck them into his mouth.

"You taste so fucking good," he said onto my lips, making me blush. I was so ready for whatever ride Rico was going to take me on.

He was perfect in my eyes, and I could see myself loving him deeply one day.

The next morning Rico and I woke up and he decided to make me go for a run. I was a dancer so running didn't bother me, but what bothered me was the getting up at five in the damn morning to do so. I could've killed him this morning when I felt his cold lips on the side of my face, waking me up as if we didn't just go to sleep. I didn't even have time to wrap my mind around the fact that I allowed him to take my virginity, and take me places my body has never been. Then after he wore my little ass out, he had the nerve to ask me to go running? I went though, it was actually pretty energizing up until I got back to the house, took a shower, then crashed in bed in my towel. In all honesty, I could get used to morning like that with him. Going to bed with him, waking up with him, I was so ready for the next step of the relationship. *Slow down, Minah, you're moving too fast*, I said to myself.

"What you over there thinking about?" Rico voice flowed through the bedroom before I actually saw him. He walked over to the bed, standing in front of me in a pair of Ethika briefs and no shirt. *Damn, he's a goddess*, I thought while licking my lips at the sight of my man.

"How tired I really am, I should've slept a little longer." I stretched while yawning. Sitting up slowly, I moved over so that he could take a seat next to me.

"It's three in the afternoon, Minah. You've slept long enough." He chuckled, making me suck my teeth. I just needed another hour of sleep. "Plus, I want to go grab something to eat and maybe go shopping in New York."

"Shopping in New York? Bet, that's all you had to say." I stuck my tongue out, making him laugh before I kissed him on his lips.

Jumping up, I darted towards the bathroom that was adjacent to his bedroom, instantly regretting it because my legs were numb. So, instead of taking a shower I prompted for a hot bubble bath to relax my muscles. About ten minutes into my bubble bath, Rico walked in naked as the day he was born and got in the shower. *Oh, I could definitely get used to this*, I thought to myself before shutting my eyes.

About ten more minutes later, I decided to get out the tub and jump in the shower with him. We washed each other up before getting out and getting dressed. Since it was damn there ninety degrees, I decided to wear a sleeveless maxi dress, with my Louis Vuitton sandals, I fixed my hair before placing my Louis Vuitton headband on my head. Applying some lip gloss to my very plain face I was satisfied. Rico met me in the bedroom dress down again, matching my style in Louis Vuitton as well. Smirking, he walked over to me kissing me softly on the lips and grabbed my hand so that we could leave.

"Which car you want to drive in today?" He asked me once we got outside, forcing a hearty laugh out of me. Looking around, my eyes stopped at his all-white Wraith and I smiled before pointing. "Good choice," was all he said before grabbing my hand and helping me into the car. About an hour and a half later, we pulled up at Gramercy Tavern, the valet helped me out the car before Rico handed him the keys.

Walking inside, he gave them his name before we were sat in a half circle booth. I loved going on dates with Rico, it was always nice and well thought out. One would think just because I was from the hood, I didn't see the finer things, but I did. Once Meen started getting money money, he had us living like royalty. My mom just wouldn't give up her home, and when he supposedly *died*, the home he purchased for her out in King of Prussia; she sold.

"I've never been here before," I said while looking over the menu.

"Me either, but I heard it was good." He shrugged making me chuckle. I loved that we always tried new things with each other.

After we ordered our food I took the time to admire him. I enjoyed everything about him, from the way he talked, ate his food, drank his water, licked his lips, stared into my soul while he talked to me. He was just all around a great man, and I was very lucky to have him in my life. Once we finish wrapping up dinner, we headed out to go shopping. He wouldn't allow me to pay for anything, he literally spoiled me and purchased me every single thing in every store we went in. I could get used to this.

"Can we walk Times Square?" I asked as we placed the last bit of my things into his car.

"Yeah, come on." He offered a smile while grabbing my hand. That's another thing about him that I admired, he always held my hand no matter where we were going. It made me feel the security of our relationship.

"You know what I noticed? You never asked me to be your girl." I inquired, being as though I never really had a boyfriend, I didn't know how this thing worked.

"I didn't know I had too, I just thought you knew you were my girl."

"Uh, boy no. I think you're supposed to ask not just assume." I sucked my teeth, making him smile showcasing those perfect teeth he has.

"Aw, babe you want to be my girl?" He stopped walking before standing in front of me. His 6'3 frame towered over my 5'8 frame before his lips made it's way to mine. "Huh, you want to be my girl?" He repeated while placing soft kisses on my lips.

"Do you want me to be your girl?" I heard myself ask. *Nice going loser*, I thought while he kept kissing me. "I mean if that's what you want, then we—" My sentence was cut short when he deepened the kiss while pulling me into him more.

"Hell yeah, I want you to be my girl. Shit, I want you to be my wife one day. I just don't want to rush you." He stared in my eyes with pure sincerity. I didn't know what to say because that's how intense his stare was, so I just nodded my head yes. "So, you my girl?" The cutest boyish grin appeared on his face.

"I guess I'm your girl." I smirked before he kissed me again, which was short lived by the vibration of his phone. He pulled his phone out before his cute face balled up, and I stood on my tippy toes to see who was calling him. Sucking my teeth, I tried to step away, but he grabbed me before kissing my forehead.

"I'ma handle it, I promise," was all he said before dragging me with him. I knew one thing he better get a handle on Kiera before I do it. Because if I have to, ain't no telling what I was going to do. But, I was going to trust my man. He said he was going to handle it, so I'm going to allow him. I needed to focus on the fact that I was finally somebody's girlfriend, I felt as if I was dreaming!

Saaleha Santana

Decisions, Decisions, Decisions.

I was finally about to take Lil' Meen to go see his dad. As much as I didn't want to, Meen was persistent. He called me every single day, sending threatening text messages which held no weight because I knew he would never do anything to hurt me. But the one threat that stuck with me was that he was going to personally call True and tell him he was alive. Even though that might be a great idea, I just thought True needed to hear it from my mouth, when I was ready. Honestly, I was still in my feelings about Ahmeen still being alive. I couldn't believe this nigga was alive after all this time, and he never thought to come for his family. All those years I spent crying, asking God why he took him from me, for his ugly ass to just be alive? I couldn't believe it. I had over a million thoughts running through my head while I packed a bag. Breaking me from my thoughts, True walked into the room, intoxicating me with his Creed cologne. Looking over my shoulder, I watched his sexy ass make his way towards me. Unintentionally, I licked my lips and smiled. Damn, I loved this man.

"Nigga, I'm pregnant like shit, and you want to be coming in here smelling like the whole damn bottle of Creed." Amber sucked her teeth, dramatically covering up her nose. She really annoys me, I swear she been milking this pregnancy thing. I can't wait until the baby comes.

"Reds, I only sprayed it twice—"

"Nigga, two times enough." She interrupted him, before rolling her eyes picking up her phone again. True laughed before turning to face me.

Different Sides Of The Game 2

"How long are you going to be gone?" True asked, sitting in front of me. For some odd reason, I wanted to cry. Cry because he was perfect. Despite the past, he was everything I wanted and needed since Meen. I couldn't believe I was in this damn predicament.

"Uh, just for the week. You won't miss me too much though; you going to be in Houston." I pouted, causing him to laugh. True and his friend Montez were going to Houston for his birthday. His birthday was last Sunday, and we spent a few days in Los Angeles, and got back yesterday. Now, it was like we were back on the road again.

"Babe, I'm going to be on my best behavior. You don't have to trip off that." He chuckled before he kissed me. "Reds, get out real quick," he said, forcing a laugh out of me. Reds looked up and rolled her eyes.

"Y'all so freaking nasty! Hurry up so I can go soak up the sun in Punta Cana." She wobbled out, making us fall out laughing.

"I can't wait until she has this baby. She so grumpy." I chuckled.

"She been grumpy. But take care of your man." He licked his lips, staring at me lustfully. "Those freaking gray eyes, man." He smirked as I dropped to my knees, pulling his joggers down, then took him whole into my mouth. He fisted my hair while I looked up at him.

"Do that thing I like," True groaned, watching me deep throat him whole. He loved when I gave him head. He always said he couldn't understand how someone so innocent could be so nasty for him. Listening to my man, I pulled his member out my mouth, making a pop noise.

"Fuck," he moaned. Licking the tip, I twirled my tongue all over it, making his body jerk before just sucking the tip while playing with his balls. I was so horny at this point. I pushed his member all the way in my mouth, swallowing him whole, and moaning as I did it. Suddenly, he pulled me up and laid me down on the bed. He lifted my dress up, ripping my panties in the process.

"Baby, wait—SHIT!!" I moaned out as he roughly entered me. I tried to move back, but couldn't when he gripped my waist and stroked deeply. "I love you!" I screamed while matching his thrust. He was so deep, he was literally taking my breath away.

"I love you more, Lee," he groaned, speeding up inside of me. After we finished, I just wanted to go to sleep. He was just that good.

"Come on, baby, get up. You gotta catch your flight." True kissed my lips. Nodding, I slowly got up. We hopped in the shower, washing each other off, then got out. I slipped on some PINK tights and a sports bra to match with a hoodie, slipped on my Chanel slides, and threw my hair in a bun. Heading down the stairs, I watched Red climb off Mack. I just knew this bitch wasn't having sex on my damn sofa!

"I know damn well you wasn't riding dick on my sofa. You could've gone to your old room!" I snapped.

"Bitch, I'm pregnant and horny! I don't give a flying fuck. When I want it, I'm hopping on it and getting it! Now let's go!" Red yelled before wobbling away. Shaking my head, my eyes traveled to Macion who was chuckle, before I shook my head.

True gave me a kiss before we headed over to get Lil' Meen from Kaylina's house. Once we got my son, we headed to the airport. I had all these mixed feelings again. I was so concerned about how Lil' Meen was going to react to his dad being alive. Here goes nothing.

"Who lives here, Mom? This house is dope!" Lil' Meen raved as soon as we pulled up to Ahmeen's estate. Taking a deep breath, I looked over at over at Amber, who was just staring at me with that 'yeah, bitch, who lives here' look. Rolling my eyes at her annoying ass, I looked back at my son.

"We're going to find out. It's a surprise, baby," was all I could muster up before climbing out the car. When we got to the door, I hesitated to knock, but leave it to Reds; she knocked for me. Sucking my teeth, she shrugged her shoulders before facing the door. About a few seconds later, the door opened, and Ahmeen's fine ass blessed us with his presence. His eyes flew to mine, before his big pink tongue brushed against his bottom lip, making me all nervous.

"Dad?" Lil' Meen questioned. "Mom, you told me he died," he said, looking up at me in disbelief. Placing my hands on his shoulders, I was about to say something, but Meen stopped me.

"What's up, Lil' Meen? Mommy did think that I was dead. Truth is, I went away to protect you guys. I'm sorry for that, but I promise to be there from here on out." I kept my hand on Lil' Meen's shoulders as he stared at his father. Then his eyes flew to mine.

"What about True?" Lil' Meen asked. He grew a relationship with True, and that was my biggest fear: taking True away, too.

"True will still be mommy's boyfriend, baby." I smiled. I loved that no matter if Ahmeen was alive or not, Lil' Meen still loved True. Lil' Meen nodded before looking up at Big Meen and smiled.

"Dad, I'm the next KD." Lil' Meen smiled, making Big Meen smile. While they spent time to bond, Reds and I roamed Meenie's mansion. Child, it was beautiful, from the marble floors, to the tall windows and high ceilings.

"Girl, I'm really about to move out here. These houses are the freak nice!" Red said, lying back on the bed. "Yeah, I'm sleeping in here; perfect view of that big ass pool. But you can't sleep with me tonight or any night we down here. Mack and I have lots and lots of phone sex when we away from each other." She smiled, making me suck my teeth.

"You such a damn nympho!" I said, forcing both of us to laugh.

"Girl, I need some dick. I can't wait to go home." Reds pouted, making me shake my head. Her ass was a mess, she literally just got some before we left.

"That's how you ended up pregnant."

"Yeah, coming from the chick that had the baby at eighteen. At least I'm twenty-seven starting." She smirked when my head snapped in her direction, then she let out a hearty laugh, making me roll my eyes.

"Bitch, that was low. You know I was a hoe for Ahmeen." I chuckled, shaking my head. "I can't believe you said that. That was Kiera low." Amber fell out laughing.

"Sis, no it wasn't." She laughed. For the rest of the night, Reds and I chilled, while Lil' Meen and Big Meen played video games and chilled. This was what I always wanted for Ahmeen Jr. his whole life. Even though he had it with True, I wanted him to have it with Meen. I honestly felt like I was dreaming. After checking on Lil' Meen, I headed upstairs to the room I picked for my stay here and decided to call True after I got out the shower. Once I got out the shower, I FaceTimed my baby.

"What's up, gray eyes?" His face appeared in the phone with the sexiest grin.

"Your neck is shining something serious. Where you going?" I smiled, forcing him to smile as well.

"Those eyes and that smile. Damn, man, I'm lucky." He licked his lips. He was just so damn perfect, I swear.

"Stop making me blush. You're such a smooth talker. Tell me what you are doing tonight?" I inquired.

"We going to that club, Levels I was telling you about that I was looking into buying from the owner. I'm basically going to check out the scene while these niggas go partying." He laughed. His teeth were so damn straight and perfect. I loved his smile.

"You're always working, baby. How about you have fun and check out the scene at the same time. And talk business tomorrow," I suggested.

"I know I'm always working and shit, babe, but—"

"Nope, no buts. I'm telling you to have fun this week. What girlfriend tells their very sexy, and I mean very sexy boyfriend to have fun in a city she's never been but knows there is some big booty hoes out there? Listen to me and have fun. You deserve it," I said sternly, making him laugh sexily.

"Big booty hoes?"

"Yes. You know Houston got those Beyoncé's." I laughed, making him chuckle too. All we did was crack jokes, corny or not. I loved our relationship.

"Nah, my Beyoncé in Punta Cana without me. So, I already got my big booty hoe." He smirked. Rolling my eyes, I stuck my tongue out.

"My booty is not that big." I mocked Lauren London from *ATL,* when she said 'my head is not that big'. He fell out laughing, shaking his head.

"You gotta chill, yo," he said in between laughter. I heard True's best friend Montez come in the room and tell him that they were leaving now. "Baby, I'm about to head out. I love you; send your boy some pictures too."

"I am not about to have your dick hard while you in somebody's club surrounded by women. Nope. I said have fun, but not too much fun." I paused when he licked his lips and smirked. "You know what, charter the jet. I'm coming to Houston."

"Baby, chill." He fell out laughing again. "It's only you, but still send me those pictures. When I get back to the hotel, if you up, we are having phone sex." He smirked, causing me to chuckle lightly while shaking my head.

"I love you, True. Byeeeee," I sang.

"I love you too, gray eyes," he said before hanging up the phone. As soon as he hung up the phone, the bathroom door opened, and in walked Ahmeen with his face all balled up.

"Why you all busting up in the bathroom like that?"

"I know you weren't talking to no nigga while you in my house," he barked, making me roll my eyes. He had some nerve.

"The only child of yours in this house is Ahmeen, Jr., so get out my face with all that bass in your tone!" I snapped, pushing past him, but he caught me by the waist. He turned me to face him, staring intensely into my eyes. At that moment, I saw nothing but pain, hurt, lust, and love in his eyes, and I was pretty sure he saw the same in mine.

"You really love him, Lee? Like you in love with him?" he asked so softly as if he was afraid of my answer. Shit, I was afraid to answer. If Ahmeen would've come back to me a year ago, I would've been all over him, but he didn't. He came back when I was starting to fall in love with someone else.

"Ahmeen, it's late..."

"Answer the question please, Saaleha," he begged.

"Yes, Ahmeen. I do love him. Am I in love with him? Not sure yet, because I've always been in love with you. Is it possible that I can fall in love with him? Yes, very possible because I've grown to love him and realized that you weren't coming back. That was my mind set, and now you're alive after hiding from me for five years. My mind is still processing all of this," was all I could say. Instead of responding, he just stared at me, not saying a word, before his hands dropped from around my waist. He nodded his head before walking out the room. I tried calling his name, but it was no use. He clearly didn't want to hear anything I had to say.

Saaleha, what are you going to do?

Ahmeen Santana

I Still Love You

♡

Saaleha had been here for about two days now, and it'd been hard as hell because I missed her. I wanted to feel her. I wanted the old Saaleha back, but she wasn't around anymore. This Saaleha that was in my home was in love with another man, and that shit was all my fault. That night I overheard her on FaceTime with True, I wanted to curse him and her out, but when I heard her say she loved him, it crushed me. It was selfish of me, but I just never thought Saaleha would move on from me. I was the one who changed her life. I was the one who she married, who she gave the baby to. I'd always hold a higher weight than True, with his disloyal ass. Then on top of this shit with Saaleha, I had to deal with Kristina's stupid ass. She went to Mexico for a few weeks because her father was sick, but she'd been calling me every single day, getting on my damn nerves.

Other than that, I was happy she brought my son to see me. He'd gotten so big and looked just like me. It fucked with me that I missed out on his life, but I had to protect my family. I had to figure out who was trying to kill me. It was just I had people shoot at me three times, I had no choice but to figure this out. The last time, I got shot up pretty good, it took me six months to recover. I needed to know who was trying to kill me and why, just to find out a bird bitch was trying to kill me. When I get my hands-on Kiera it's over for her. But for now, I needed to rekindle with my family; that was more important to me. I'd catch Kiera real soon.

Walking into my room, Saaleha was standing in my bedroom with a picture of us in her hand. That was my favorite picture of us. She was pregnant and was mad at me for talking about how she looked. I used to just mess with her because she'd get so mad, she would say I antagonized her; it was just so easy. *Damn, I miss those days,* I thought as I watched her before speaking.

"I remember that day like it was yesterday, at the baby shower. We were just arguing before that because I called—"

"You called me fat for like the millionth time since I was pregnant." Saaleha interrupted me, making me chuckle. "You were so rude," she said softly, shaking her head, then picked up another picture of us with Lil' Meen. "This was two days before you got shot..." she said softly. That also was my favorite picture.

"Red caught the moment." I chuckled. "I called her a fake photographer and you know her hype ass responded like..."

"Don't do me, nigga," we said in unison. Saaleha shook her head and put the frame down. Looking up in the mirror, we connected eyes, making me realize she was crying. I never meant to hurt her.

"Five years. Five years you've been alive, and you never told me or sent one thing to give me hope that you were returning," she said softly, staring at me through the mirror. I strolled over to her, forcing her to put her hand up to tell me to stop, but fuck that. I was tired of her pushing me to the side. I continued to walk up on her, then I turned her around, picking her up and placing her on the dresser. A nigga's heart was racing as we stared into each other's eyes. I saw all the love she had for me in hers. After all these years, she still loved me the same.

"Back up," she said, breaking my train of thought.

"No," I said while touching her face, causing her eyes to shut. "I know I fucked up not coming home sooner; I did that to protect my family. Babe, you don't get it. Niggas wanted me dead—"

"So, for five years, you chose to deal with it by abandoning your family?" she interrupted me before sucking her teeth. She pushed me a little, but I didn't budge. "Then on top of that, you thought I wasn't going to notice that you got a whole bitch, bro?"

"W-what are you talking about, Pocahontas?" I stuttered, staring at her while she read me. Rolling her eyes, she chuckled a little before shaking her head.

"You got heels by your door, lingerie in the top drawer, and women clothes in your closet. Now, unless you drag queening it, my nigga, I say you got a girl." She cocked her head to the side, awaiting my answer. I didn't know what to say, so I shrugged. She chuckled before pushing me back again, but I gripped her thighs. "You so full of shit!"

"Pocahontas, I'm—"

"Stop calling me that! That girl died right along with you. Five years ago! I'm not trying to hear I'm sorry, none of that shit, Ahmeen. I want to know what the fuck happened that you had to abandon me and your son." She snapped. Taking a step back, I took a look at my wife and finally noticed the change. This wasn't the girl I fell in love with ten years ago; this wasn't the girl I married. This was the new Saaleha, the one who had to learn to live without me, who had to learn to survive without me, the one I broke.

Taking a deep breath, I spoke. "Man, remember that nigga Ronnie?" After she registered on who I was talking about, her pretty face balled up in disgust.

"Ewe, my neighbor Ronnie from the Bottom?" she asked while I nodded my head. "Yeah. I remember his annoying ass; he used to stalk me."

"Well yeah, him. He a part of some Jamaican cartel that's ran by his uncle, who I happened to know. I used to do business with them, but I'm guessing since Ronnie's ass is hating off me, he gotta stick by blood. Them niggas was supposed to kill me that night and got Kiera to handle it because they were fucking. He told me everything when I talked to him a few weeks ago."

"My Kiera? She wouldn't do no foul shit like that, Ahmeen. He lied to you." She instantly defended Kiera, like she always did.

"Lee, when you going to learn that she not truly happy for you? She never was. She tried her hand with me, with Mack. She not loyal."

"Okay, but that doesn't mean she'll try to kill you. She wouldn't do that to me, no. I'm her best friend, she—"

"Saaleha, baby! Open your damn eyes! Stop being so fucking naïve, shawty! She's not no friend of yours! She wants your life; she wanted your life since you were a pup. Baby, you gotta stop being so naïve when it comes to people. Stop thinking people wouldn't do something, because they would. You can't put shit past anybody, not even me, baby girl," I barked, making her flinch. I hated that Saaleha was so naïve. She would always try to see the good in people instead of accepting the fact that they would hurt her.

"I am not naïve. I just don't think she would do that, Ahmeen." She sighed, looking off to the side. Shaking my head, I chuckled.

"She would do that; she did do that. Her and that nigga Omar took everything from me."

"They didn't take everything from you, Ahmeen—"

"They didn't? My wife! My fucking wife, who I made vows with, won't even let me touch her without flinching. My damn wife is in love with another nigga because these niggas wanted to play with my life! I lost everything, you can't—"

"No!" She pushed me away from her. "You don't get to do that, stupid! Your stupid ass decided to play dead! *You,* stupid mother—" I ceased all her yelling with a kiss. A deep kiss that she melted into, until she pushed me away. "Ahmeen..."

"Naw, shut up and listen. I played dead because your dad told me to! They were coming after you and my son if I didn't presume dead. They wanted to take everything from me. They wanted to hurt me. And if I didn't supposedly die, they would've made sure you and Lil' Meen did. I did this shit for you!" I barked.

"No bitch, you did this shit for yourself! I don't care! I hate you so much! I suffered five years, crying every damn day, telling my son his dad was never returning! Now look at your stupid ass, alive and breathing! I'm pissed off with you. You such a dumb bitch! Why did I even go down North that day!" she screamed with tears flooding down her face.

"Naw, you ain't mean that shit. You just mad. It's cool." I chuckled before shaking my head. "Yeah, you just mad." I nodded before turning around to walk away.

Different Sides Of The Game 2

"Ahmeen."

"Naw, Saaleha, I'm sorry for hurting you the worst way possible. But I had to do what I had to do to protect my family." I shrugged, walking into the bathroom, leaving her standing there. Never, no matter how mad she got, had she ever regretted meeting me. Saaleha said a lot of shit when she was mad, but for some reason, I believed her. Stepping in the shower, I let the hot water cascade on me, stuck in my thoughts. Feeling like someone was watching me, I turned around and saw Saaleha standing at the shower door, eyes filled with lust, biting her bottom lip. I turned around, with my dick facing her and all. Her eyes flew down to my member, and she bit her lip harder.

"You going to stand there or get in with me so I can give you some of your dick?" I asked her, making her eyes fly to my face. Her head dropped back, making me chuckle.

"Ahmeen." She pouted, stomping her foot. "I have a boyfriend."

"Technically, you have a husband and a boyfriend. We never got a divorce," I responded before walking toward her, thinking she was going to move, but she didn't. Pulling the bottom of her dress, I demanded, "Take the shit off before I take it off for you." She shook her head, forcing me to pull her into the shower with me. Picking her up, I walked her under the shower head.

"Ahmeen!" she yelled, causing me to chuckle before kissing her soft ass lips. Lifting her dress over her head, she fought me while I kissed and sucked on her tongue. When my finger made contact with her clit, she ceased all movement. Ripping her panties off, she gripped my back as I took off the rest of her clothes.

"Let me take care of you," was all I said before hemming her to the shower wall and entering her. I hadn't felt her in five long years, and I never missed her more than I did now. She fit me like a glove, like she was made for me. I didn't care what she said, she was mine.

"Fuck, Ahmeen, stop... Wait," she moaned into my mouth, as I stroked her on her G-spot, just how she loved me to.

"You really want me to?" I asked, kissing on her neck. Pulling away, I looked at her face, which displayed the cutest sex face. "Huh,

Different Sides Of The Game 2

Pocahontas? You want me to stop?" Biting her bottom lip, she opened her eyes, and shook her head. "Nah, you know I need you to talk, baby." I slowed my strokes down.

"Don't stop," she said softly while staring at me. Our connection was still strong. I felt her heart beating through my body. "Kiss me," she requested, and I did so while I picked up my strokes.

"Fuck, man. I miss the fuck out of you." I groaned in her mouth before I placed a hand on the wall above her head, cuffing her ass and deepening my strokes. I missed the way Saaleha felt and how she would make me feel.

"Damn," Saaleha moaned out as she came hard on my dick.

"I'm sorry, Lee... damn... Man, I love you," I moaned, speeding up my movements. She bounced on my dick as I gripped her waist, then she clenched her muscles, knowing I wouldn't last. "Shit, baby... You still don't play fair," I moaned, making her smile.

"I love you too, Meen," she moaned as she came on my dick, and I shot the club up. After we got our breathing together, I slipped out of her and helped her to her feet. She stared me in my eyes with a look I couldn't make out, before she grabbed her wet clothes and walked out of the shower.

What the hell was we going to do now? I thought to myself.

Amber "Reds" Wright

Don't Let the Necessary Occur

Ever since Ahmeen called himself faking his death, I'd been spending all of my time with Saaleha. She'd been going crazy, literally, unsure if she should tell True, and what he would think. Then, on top of her being hurt, when we were in DR, she had sex with Meen, making things harder than they already were. Her naïve ass. My sis was going through a lot. I was so happy we were back home though. Spending my time with her was very easy while Macion was away, but now since his cry baby ass was home, I had to balance my time between them.

Lately, things with Mack and I had been great. After finding out delusional ass Cherelle's baby wasn't his, we've moved into a great place. I was almost due and so ready to get this baby out of me. She sat on my bladder, all day, every day, causing me to always have to pee. Mack had been very hands on with me and my pregnancy. I think we were just both happy as hell to be finally having a baby. After trying for four long years, hearing doctors tell me they didn't know why I couldn't get pregnant, we were now finally about to have our own baby. I couldn't have been any happier.

I had just left from getting me something to eat from California Pizza Kitchen, and on my way back to the house. Noticing I hadn't talked to Saaleha since early this morning, I decided to hit her up.

"Hello." Saaleha's voice flowed through the speakers of my car.

"What you doing?" I asked while switching lanes, noticing this black 2013 Chevy Malibu had been following me since I left out of the parking lot.

"I'm at Gucci, about—"

"Bitch, we banned Gucci. What is you doing?" I interrupted her, making her laugh deeply.

"Shut up. I'm returning some things for True. I guess he's banning them too." She laughed before she got quiet. "I really love him, Reds. What am I going to do?" I heard the stress in her voice. I knew that this was messing with her.

"I don't know, sis, but I'm here for—" I paused when I noticed the car still following while I was on the highway.

"Hello," I heard Lee's voice boom through the speakers, with shaky hands I switched lanes, and the car did the same thing.

"Sis, someone is following me," I said.

"What? Where are you? Hold on. I'm about to call Mack," was all she said before the line got quiet. Who could've been following me? This was the part of dating someone who used to be in the streets that I hated. You never really knew who was after your man, and you knew niggas nowadays went after your family.

"Babe, what's the color of the car that's following you?" Mack's voice flowed through the car speakers.

"It's a black Chevy Malibu, like the one I had back in 2013. It's tinted, so I can't see," I whined. "And now the baby is kicking," I said in panic.

"You got your bracelet on, right?" he asked, referring to the Cartier bracelet he purchased me for my twenty-first birthday. I didn't know it had a tracking device in it, until I called myself breaking up with him, and he popped up. I was so mad at him for it, but at this moment, I was happy as hell I had this damn thing on.

"Yes... ahhhhh! They hit my car!" I yelled.

"Reds!" Mack and Saaleha yelled into the phone before the line disconnected. Me, on the other hand, my head hit the window, causing everything to go black.

When I finally came to, I was in an abandoned building, and was tied to a chair. Looking around, I tried to recognize something, but I couldn't. On top of all this bullshit, I was having major contractions. Looking down at my jeans, I noticed I had an entire wet spot on the front. My damn water broke; perfect. I looked around the abandoned building, trying not to cry, but damn these contractions were killing me.

"Help me!" I yelled out, and the response I received made me cringe.

"Oh, shut up, bitch. Nobody can hear you." Cherelle chuckled as she walked around the corner. It was that moment that I realized that Cherelle was certified, truly. She walked towards me with her pupils dilated, looking as if she was on some type of drugs. Cherelle tried to give me some water, but I turned my head away. I was not trusting shit from her crazy ass. "It's just water, bitch. You are pregnant. I'm not trying to kill the baby. But I am going to cut that baby out of you, kill you, and move on happily ever after with Mack."

"You are the dumbest bitch alive, Cherelle. Un-fucking tie me now!" I yelled out, making Cherelle laugh deeply, sending chills down my spine for the first time ever in my life.

"I'm not doing shit, bitch. You ruined my life. You know my husband left me and took my got damn son with him! I don't even know where he is, and Mack won't even answer my calls because of you, bitch. You took him from me!" Cherelle yelled with tears streaming down her face. This bitch was really crazy. I was going to kill Macion's stupid ass, I swear. I stared at this psycho, baffled that I really underestimated Cherelle's mental state. *This was some real Thin Line Between Love and Hate shit, seriously.* I thought as I stared up at her, baffled.

"Cherelle, I've been with Mack my entire life. I didn't take him from no—shit!" I yelled out when another contraction ripped through. They were like six minutes apart now. "Cherelle, come on. Take me to the hospital, please. Don't do this."

"Fuck you. I'm not taking you nowhere. You took him from me! You just had to interrupt what me and Mack had going on. He loved me! He told me on multiple occasions! He told me he actually gave a fuck about me, and if I never came there that day, he would've still been fucking with me!" Cherelle yelled out. Crazy part, I knew Mack had love for this girl. I knew he loved her. I knew it that night she popped up at our home, pregnant. I saw it all in his face.

"You want him? You can have him. I couldn't care less. I'm pregnant, and my baby is coming, Cherelle! Please just take me to the hospital!" I cried out.

"It hurts, doesn't it? I thought I was going to die, girl." Cherelle chuckled as if something was funny. I just stared at her long and hard. This bitch was really crazy. "But I'm not taking you nowhere! We going to have this baby, and I'm taking it away from you and living with Mack, because he loves me! And as long as you're out the picture, he'll love me easily!" Cherelle snapped.

"Cherelle, what the fuck are you doing!" Mack yelled as Ahmeen and Jay walked in behind him with their guns drawn. Cherelle's eyes flew to Ahmeen's, before her mouth opened and closed.

"Omar killed... I thought you were—"

"Fuck all that. What the fuck are you doing!" Macion interrupted her.

"I'm getting rid of her so we can live happily! She ruined my life, so I'm ruining hers. You love me, Mack!" Cherelle screamed.

"Shawty, what's his real name?" Ahmeen asked with his face balled up.

"It's Mack!" Cherelle yelled, making Meen and Jay suck their teeth. This bitch really was dumb, crazy, and clueless. I swear, Macion sure did know how to pick them.

"Bitch, no it's not. He doesn't love you for real, ma." Jay chuckled. Cherelle looked at Mack, confused.

"Ahhhh!" I cried out as another contraction ripped through. I knew one thing, if they didn't get me to the hospital as soon as possible, everybody was going to feel my wrath.

"Oh, bitch, shut up. Labor don't hurt that bad!" Cherelle yelled before turning back to face the boys. *She's so tough while I'm tied up*, I thought to myself while staring at her.

"Shit, yes the fuck it does. Lee was about to kill my ass. Bro, you better handle this bitch so we can get sis to the hospital," Ahmeen said, making Jay shake his head, but laugh.

"Macion, do something!" I yelled out. Mack looked up at me as tears flowed out of my eyes. This shit was all his fault. If he could have just kept his damn dick to himself, we wouldn't be in this damn predicament!

"I love you, Mack. Why can't you see that? I'll kill this bitch if I have to." Cherelle whined as she walked toward me with her gun pointed at my head. I couldn't believe Macion didn't kill her yet.

"This that *Thin Line Between Love or Hate*. Kill her ass." Ahmeen shook his head.

"I was thinking the same shit." I mumbled, wondering what was taking Mack so long. "You love her, don't you?" I asked.

"Of course he does. He's in—"

"Don't you?" I yelled out, interrupting her. I stared at Mack with tears flowing down my eyes. I stared at the man that I always only loved, in disbelief that he actually loved someone else.

"Reds, I had love for her, but I didn't love her," he said before pointing his gun directly at Cherelle, but Ahmeen shot her in the stomach.

"What the fuck!" Mack yelled out, making Ahmeen suck his teeth.

"Finish the bitch, man. We gotta get sis to the hospital. We don't have time for this shit!" Ahmeen barked, making Jay chuckle. Mack shook his head before walking up on Cherelle. He really loved this bitch.

"We were supposed to be forever... I love you," Cherelle said, right before Mack let off three shots to her head.

"Damn." Jay shook his head before he pulled out his phone to contact their clean-up crew. Ahmeen helped me out of the chair. When Mack went to touch me, I snatched away from him before punching him in the face.

"On bro, if this little girl wasn't coming, I would be killing you with that bitch!" I yelled while pushing him out my way. Ahmeen and Jay were snickering the whole time. Those two irked my soul more than anything. When I finally got to the hospital, I was fully dilated and ready to push my beautiful baby out. About ten minutes later, we welcomed Amaya Madison Dupree, into this crazy world. They always say, when someone dies, someone is born.

Jayceon "Jay" Johnson
You Will Always Be

It'd been a few days since Mack had to kill ol' girl, and my niece, Amaya, was born. We'd all been spending a lot of time over there, except Meen, because he had to head back to Dominican Republic the same day Cherelle died. Mack had been stressing though because Reds hadn't really been speaking to him and shit. He thought she was going through that postpartum shit, but me knowing Amber, she was upset with him about Cherelle. Other than that, we all were happy as hell Meen was finally back. Except Saaleha. I didn't blame her either, because she had to live life thinking he wasn't alive. She even tried to physically fight Mack and me when she found out that we knew Meen was alive. Her little crazy ass.

Let me formally introduce myself since I really didn't have a part in part one. I'm Jayceon, but everybody calls me Jay. At twenty-seven, I was a multi-millionaire. Being a nigga from Highbridge, I never really thought I'd be living life like this, running my own businesses and shit. I stood about six feet four, caramel complexion, with ginger colored hair, deep brown eyes, and freckles on my face; I hated them. I had tattoos from my neck down, I lived and breathed art. Half of them I did myself. A lot of people said I favored the bull CLD Toon, but I didn't see it. When I moved to Philly, a lot of niggas used to think I was a pretty boy, until I had to fight. That was how Meen, Mack, and I became cool. People used to test me all the time, as if I didn't kill niggas for less, and make them disappear like they never existed. Anyway, I was out at Paprika, about to get something to eat, before I headed to my crib out Elkins Park.

"Jayceon?" Her sweet, familiar voice broke my train of thought. Turning around, I was face to face with the girl I fell in love with a year ago, Khyreema. She still looked good, from her blemish free, deep chocolate complexion, to her almond shape brown eyes, and perfect, straight white teeth that brought out her complexion when she smiled. She had her natural hair out, which was big and curly. I loved that shit better than those wigs she be wearing. I hadn't seen her in months, since I had to leave her ass.

"What's up, Khy?" I said, cocking my head to the side. Before she got to say anything, Kaylina came running up and jumping into my arms. Chuckling, I kissed her forehead before pulling away. "What's up, Kay Kay? You been being good for mommy?"

"Yesssss... I miss you, Jay Jay. Can you hang out with me and Mommy today?" she asked, making me smile because she was perfect, looking just like her mom with a lighter complexion. I looked over at Khy, who shrugged her shoulders.

"Yeah, I'll spend some time with you, only if mommy buys me food," I said while we both turned to look at Khy. She chuckled before nodding her head. "Well, let's go."

"Mommy, I'm driving with Jay Jay. I miss his Tesla." She jumped out of my arms before tugging me toward my car. This little girl could talk me into anything. Back when I first met Khyreema, I always wanted Kaylina as my daughter. She was the perfect kid, honestly.

After we got to Khyreema's house out the county, we ate dinner just like old times. I didn't know how much I missed them until now. I just tucked Kaylina into bed, then headed into the kitchen to let Khy know I was out. Khyreema had changed her clothes into a pair of shorts and an oversized t-shirt; it was mine. Clearing my throat, she turned around, looking up at me. She wore a small smile, but when she noticed that I wasn't smiling, hers dropped.

"I'm out," I said. She nodded slowly, before looking down at nothing in particular. Then her pretty eyes found mine, and she sighed.

"Can we talk first?" she asked, while I sucked my teeth. "Jayceon, please. I'll talk, and you just listen, please." I nodded my head, then took a seat at her kitchen table. I could tell she was surprised by my answer because I usually gave her the cold shoulder, but it'd been long enough since we last spoke.

"You going to talk or stare at a nigga?"

"You don't have to be rude. You used to be so nice to me. I wish—"

"Yeah, until you did some nut shit," I interrupted her, as she rolled her eyes then pouted. She went to touch my hand, but I moved it. "Talk, Khy."

"Jayceon, I'm sorry. How many times do I have to say it?"

"If you never did it, then—"

"Then what? Huh? You seriously think us having our baby would've been a good time? You got a whole ass girlfriend that you're not leaving! You thought I was going to settle for you jumping back and forth between the both of us? Because you are mistaking love for loyalty; shit, barely even loyalty, because we both know that bitch be going out nutty!" she spat. Her chest heaved up and down, while her eyes stared into mine. "The problem is, you wanted me to be a dumb bitch. Well, baby, I can't. I'm a whole ass mother, and my daughter needs stability. No matter how much she loves your ass, the shit you still have going with Rhonda isn't enough for me or my daughter."

It's crazy how after all this time, I was still in love with her. I met Khyreema a year ago at Saaleha's shop. When I saw her chocolate ass, I wanted her. I didn't give a damn about Rhonda's ghetto ass either. I needed and wanted Khy. After a lot of chasing, I finally got her, well forced her, to go on a date with me. It was all downhill from there. We spent mad time together, but of course I had a girl, who basically became my side bitch. I would never ask Khyreema to be my side anything. Anyway, I spent time jumping between the two, up until Khy got pregnant with my seed. Everything about her being pregnant made me want to leave Rhonda for good, but the other part was that Rhonda had been down with me since I was nineteen. I wasn't in love with her. I was in love with Khyreema, but because Rhonda was loyal to me, I stayed. I stayed when I knew I should've been with Khy. Khyreema, being the strong chick, she was, got tired of me jumping back and forth and ended things. But when she ended things with me, she ended everything. She killed my seed.

I had never wanted to lay a hand on her so bad, until that day. I was so pissed with her, as she stood in her house, screaming and crying. But I wasn't trying to hear that shit. I wanted my baby, especially with Khyreema's ass. I had it all planned out when she told me she was pregnant. No matter how uncertain I was, I wanted this family shit with her ass. After that, I left her, blocked her, and stopped coming around the shop. Our shit was a secret anyway, but I didn't need Saaleha or hype ass Reds pressing me over this shit.

"Jay—"

"I don't know what you want me to say, Khy. You knew what you signed up for. I wasn't—"

"No! Don't do that to me! Don't shut me out because you're mad at me; it's me you're talking to. I'm sorry. I'm so freaking sorry that I hurt you, but what did you expect me to do?"

"I expected you to have my fucking baby instead of being a weak bitch and get an abortion! You keep screaming out Rhonda, as if she would've come before my seed! My fucking seed that you killed behind some bitch that knows you exist, that knows I'm in love with your ass. You did that shit! Not me." I hated that she was the only person who could take me here. Get me in my feelings over some old shit that I honestly wasn't over. We sat there staring at each other, while tears fell from her eyes. "Listen, I'm out. Tell Kay I love her and that I'll come get her soon, if it's cool with you."

Nodding her head, she wiped her face, standing up, then walked out the kitchen. I took a deep breath before I stood and followed behind her. She was already at the door, with it open. I stood in front of her before pulling her into me, hugging her tightly.

"I just wish you understand that I'm in love with you and I want this, too. And I'm truly sorry. You can come get Kay whenever you want," she mumbled into my chest. Pulling away, I looked down at her before kissing her forehead.

"I'll hit you up," was all I said before I headed out the door. I loved Khy with all of me, but I didn't know if I was ready to forgive her. I needed to get away from her, but how was I going to do that again, when I already made promises to Kaylina? And on top of all this, I was still dealing with Rhonda's ratchet ass.

Ain't this some shit.

"Where the hell have you been? I've been calling you all day!" Rhonda screamed as soon as I walked through her apartment doors. She stood there in a pair of PINK shorts, with a sports bra. Rhonda was your typical around the way girl, with her light skin complexion and perfect body. She wasn't too stacked but was way thicker than Khyreema's small frame. Rhonda reminded me of Lira Galore, just lighter.

"Man, go 'head with all that shit, yo." I pushed past her, taking a seat on her sofa.

"What you mean, go 'head with all that shit? Nigga, where you been at! You've been ignoring me for a few days too, so tell me what's up!" she yelled. Dropping my head back, I realized I was tired of this arguing shit. I mean a huge part of it was my fault, but another huge part was her fault too. I was over this shit, and after seeing Khyreema, I was really over it.

"You know I be out handling business. I was—"

"So, your businesses more important than me?" she interrupted. This girl gotta be stupid, I thought as I stared at her.

"Rhonda, is you stupid or is you dumb? Nothing is more important than my money. You out of... you know what? I don't got time for this shit. I'm out. I'll hit you up." I shook my head before standing up. Panic flashed in her eyes as she jumped in front of me.

"I'm sorry, I just... Baby, I just missed you. I'm sorry." This was another thing. Rhonda was weak willed. I hated that shit.

Shaking my head, I removed her hands from my shirt and walked around her. I heard her calling my name and shit, and honestly, tonight she didn't even do anything for me to leave. Khyreema's words kept replaying in my head, that she was in love with me. That she wanted this too. Jumping inside of my Tesla Model S, I headed back to where my heart always was and always had been. When I finally pulled up, I parked in the driveway behind her Nissan Altima. Getting out the car, I knocked on the door and waited for her to open the door. She answered the door in her robe, with her hair up in a ponytail. She stared at me for a little before she unlocked the screen door.

"Is everything okay?" she asked before stepping to the side to let me in, but I didn't move. I needed to know something before I stepped foot into her house, into her life again. "Jayc—"

"You're in love with me?" I interrupted. She stared at me for a little before nodding her head. "You want this shit between us to work?" Again, she nodded her head. "Can you forgive me for my mistakes, and I'll forgive you for yours, and we move on from the past?"

"I been forgave you, Jay." She spoke so sincerely. I didn't know what else to say, so I stared at her. Nodding my head, I picked her up, kissing her, and she instantly wrapped her legs around me. "No more Rhonda?"

"She's done," I said in between kisses. Khyreema pulled away, searching my eyes, before the cutest smile blessed her face. "I promise, Khy." Knowing she was going to ask me to promise her, she chuckled before kissing me again.

"I love you, Jayceon."

"I love you too," was all I said before I carried her to her bedroom. I knew Rhonda wasn't going be cool with me moving on especially with Khyreema, but as long as I had Khy in my corner, I was good. We were good.

Khyreema would always be mine.

Ahmeen Santana

Still Goin' Bad

"I know you didn't just say you moving back to the States!" Kristina yelled. After Saaleha came up here with my son, I promised my son he'd see me more. I wouldn't be able to keep that promise from the Dominican Republic. I already missed five years of his life; I didn't plan on missing more. Then on top of that, Saaleha's ass was still with True, so I really needed to be around. Ain't no nigga playing daddy to my kid.

"You knew this day was coming, Kris. I need to be closer to my son." I shrugged while I continued to pack my bags. "You can keep the crib, though." I was tired of traveling back and forth to be around my family and shit. And I was tired of Saaleha keeping me a secret to her nigga, talking about when the time was right. I would give her time, but I needed her to hurry up.

"The crib? Are you serious right now, Meen?" Kristina pouted. I didn't know what she wanted me to do or say. I was leaving. "Meen, baby. It's me. You love me, I—"

"I do not love you. Don't be adding shit." I barked, stopping what I was doing. I didn't know what her damn problem was. Love her? That was a little extreme. "Aren't you in love with True?" When I said his name, her eyes widened. Yeah, I knew about her thing with True. That day Mack and Jay were here and they saw her, they knew exactly who she was. I guessed from being around True.

"W-what— how do you know about True?" She stuttered before taking a seat on the bed. Her brown eyes were trained on mine, while I just stared at her. She really underestimated me and my pull. I knew everything; I found out everything.

"That's not what I asked you. Aren't you in love with him?"

"N-no, I just—"

"You were just fucking him behind my back and thought I was never going to find out, right?" I cocked my head to the side, waiting for her to answer, but the only answer I got was her fake ass tears. "You funny, scrap."

Ignoring her fake ass tears, I continued to pack the rest of my things. Saaleha's dad, Dom, was waiting for me at the clear port with his private jet. He was coming to the states with me because, according to Saaleha, we had some explaining to do. Her mom had already flown out, and Saaleha wanted all of us to tell her the truth. It was the least I could do. She knew my truth but not how I knew her dad or how he got involved. Once I finished packing the rest of my things, I stopped in front of Kristina, who was still crying. *This girl should've been an actress*, I thought. Her eyes traveled up to mine, and she reached out to hug me, and I didn't stop her.

"Please don't leave me," she mumbled into my shirt. Shaking my head, I pulled away from her. "What do I have to do? I don't want to lose you, Ahmeen." When she said my name, her accent came out. I'm telling y'all, I loved a bitch with an accent. I thumbed her tears away before kissing her lips softly.

"I was never yours to keep, ma." I whispered against her lips before I pulled away. Her mouth was ajar; she actually looked astounded. Smirking, I turned around, grabbed my bags, and headed for the bedroom door. "The crib and cars are yours, baby!" I yelled as I continued to the stairs.

"You're going to regret leaving me!" Kristina yelled behind me. "I can't believe that y'all keep picking that… that, *puta*, over me! She has nothing on me! I held both of y'all down, and what the fuck did she do?" I chuckled at her little rant. As I made it to the door, I felt her right on my back. Turning around quickly, she jumped back while fear flashed across her face.

"How am I going to regret leaving you?" I asked, walking up on her, backing her into the table that was placed in the middle of the walkway. "I don't take to threats easily, baby girl. So, what's good?"

"Nothing, baby. I just—please don't go."

"You going out nutty, ma." I chuckled before taking a step back. I took Kristina in one last time before I turned around and opened the door. "Take care though," was all I said before I left out the door. I knew Kristina, and I knew what she was capable of. I would be keeping an eye on her. I knew I shouldn't have messed with a bitch in a cartel; they be slower than regular hood bitches. I wasn't worried though, because if it came down to it, I wouldn't hesitate to put a hot one in her dome.

"So, your rude ass just going to have us waiting for hours like that?" Saleemah said as soon as Saaleha walked in the door. Saaleha rolled her eyes before sitting her Birkin bag down on the coffee table and sat down next to me.

"I do have a career that doesn't stop because now y'all shady asses want to talk." She rolled her eyes, forcing a chuckle out of me. Her ass was so feisty. She looked over at me and laughed lightly.

"Little girl, don't get cute, because I'll knock your ass right out." Saleemah stood up, but Dom grabbed her arm to pull her back down. "No, she knows I don't play that shit."

"She's just angry, give—"

"So, this how it's going to be? Let me know now. She's been dying to be a daddy's girl." Saleemah interrupted Dom, making me fall out laughing because she wasn't lying. Saaleha childish ass stuck her tongue out at her mom, making Saleemah try to lunge at her. "I'm going to get you, watch. Your ass ain't too old to get beat."

"Ard, Mom, dang, chill. I'm sorry for being late. I really was working." Saaleha whined like the big baby she was. "So how do you know my dad, Meenie?" Hearing her call me Meenie made me smile because I hadn't heard it in years. Even though I hated that gay ass name, I loved hearing her say it.

"Princess, he didn't know I was your father until he got shot up that night," Dom answered instead. Saaleha's eyes traveled to his, and she stared at him. "But, I always knew he was your husband. I knew who he was before y'all started dating, but when y'all did start dating, I made it my business to get to know him. I didn't want him to know he was messing with the bosses' daughter, because then he would've probably started acting different. I wanted to know him. I wanted to know what he was about, no front."

"How did you know he even know about——" She paused and looked at her mom. "You told him?"

"Girl, no. When I finally did, he already knew about him," Saleemah sassed.

"All your life, I kept a close eye on you. I'm pretty sure your mom told you about why I wasn't in your life. I knew that her dad not speaking to her was killing her, so I removed myself. When I tried to still be around on the low up until you were two, your grandpop found out and cut your mother off. So, I distanced myself. I kept in contact with your mom, but I couldn't see you. I don't want you to think I didn't want you or your mom. I did it to protect you." He stopped talking when he noticed Saleemah was crying. He grabbed her hand and kissed it. You could see all the love between them.

"Why does everyone keep saying they do things to protect me? I can protect myself. I've been protecting myself since I was a kid. I can handle the truth!" Saaleha yelled. If it was possible, her bronze skin tone was almost red.

"Because, baby, you can be naïve about things sometimes. Just how you always thought Kiera——"

"This shit isn't about Kiera! I know she wouldn't hurt me like y'all did." Saaleha interrupted Saleemah, who scoffed at Lee. I didn't know why she thought Kiera wouldn't hurt her. That thot was at the top of the list.

"See what I mean by naïve? That girl has always been jealous of you and Amber. It was like it came out of nowhere too. But I won't sit here and say she's always been the same; it started a little bit before you met Meen. You'll learn though, if you haven't by now." Saleemah shook her head.

Saaleha nodded her head before standing. She reached out for my hand, and I grabbed hers. We walked to the backyard before taking a seat at the table that was on the deck. We didn't say anything for the first couple minutes; I wanted her to digest everything she just heard. It was the same thing I had to do when her dad told me. It was crazy how somebody could really be watching you and you have no clue.

"Is it bad of me that I want Ronnie dead?" she started before looking at me. "Is it bad that I want him dead for taking you away from me?" Her voice cracked at the end before a lone tear fell out of her right eye. "Is it crazy that even though I don't want to believe Kiera would do something like this to me, I know she did?"

"You don't have to worry about Ronnie. I handled him already." Her eyes flew to mine because she knew exactly what I meant. "As for Kiera, don't worry about her; she going to get what's coming for her. Trust me."

"Can I be there when you get her? I need to know why she did it," she asked, and I nodded my head. "And since we killing her and all that, can I be the one to pull the trigger?"

"Saaleha, you not built for shit like that. I can't—"

"Please? She was supposed to be my best friend. She took you from me, Ahmeen. I have to do this." She practically begged me; I didn't know what to say. So, I said the only thing that I knew would get her to move past this conversation.

"I'll think about it, and when the time comes, make sure you're by the phone." The grin that appeared on her face made me laugh. "You're so weird."

"Put it on *piru*." She smirked, making me shake my head; her fake wannabe down ass.

"You don't even know what that mean."

"Uh hunh; people in red uniforms," she said matter-of-factly. I shook my head because I did not expect her green ass to know what that meant.

"Oh, my fault, blood." The smile on her face made a nigga's heart flutter... cute ass.

"I never been so excited to do some shit like—" She paused before her eyes widened.

"What?"

"I'm going have to pray because I don't have time, I need to make into the heaven gates," her stupid ass said, making me laugh. "That's not funny. This some gangsta ass shit. Whew, baby. Kiera better watch her back."

She wasn't lying either; Kiera better watch her back. Because when I finally caught her, it was going to be lights out for her.

Later that night….

"Pocahontas, I wish you turn this shit off," I mumbled.

"Mom! Come on, man. Me and Dad don't want to watch this corny show." Lil' Meen whined as we were chilling in my living room. I chuckled at his little face balled up, just thinking how much he was my twin.

"I can't believe you still watch this bullshit." I mumbled before she popped my leg and laughed. After all these years, her ratchet ass still was watching *Love & Hip Hop.* Then to make matters worse, this shit expanded to Miami and Hollywood. I didn't know none of these niggas on the Miami one, except Trick Daddy, Trina's fine ass, and Gunplay.

"I missed this episode on Wednesday. Shut up you two. It's going off in like ten minutes, then we can find a movie to watch," she said, never removing her eyes from the television. Me and Lil' Meen both gave her that 'yeah, right' look before our eyes connected.

"Are you going to cook though? I'm starving!" Lil' Meen asked his mom.

"We can order some Mexican food. I mean, if that's still your favorite?" I asked Saaleha, forcing her eyes to linger over to mine.

Her face held a weird expression before she smiled softly and focused back on the TV.

"Yup, it's both of our favorite, Dad."

"Or, you could go in the kitchen and make your famous spicy mango chicken," Saaleha suggested with the cutest grin on her face. "See Meen, your dad used to make me spicy mango chicken almost every day, and I just think you would love it. Shouldn't he make it?"

"Yeah, Dad! You should make some, with some white rice and spinach."

"Spinach? Your mom turned you soft, kid." I chuckled when Lee's little hand punched me in my side. "What? I'm just—"

"Nah, Dad. I'm a basketball player. I have to eat right sometimes," Lil' Meen interrupted, making Saaleha stick her tongue out at me. My little nigga was smart as hell. I couldn't believe I missed out on this right here. Doing as my family asked, I got up and headed into the kitchen to thaw some chicken out. Once the chicken was thawed, I started up cooking. I had been cooking for about twenty minutes before Lee came into my kitchen.

"Do you need help?" Her sweet voice flowed through my kitchen. I turned around and smiled before shaking my head. "You sure? I'm just—"

"Pocahontas, I got this." I licked my lips, watching her eyes fly to them. Then she threw her hands up in a surrendering way, before she backed out of the kitchen. When she turned around, I couldn't help to look at her ass; that thing was sitting. About fifteen minutes later, I finished up dinner, and for the first time ever, I sat at the dinner table with my wife and son. Shit felt good. I felt like a family man, which pushed me more to want to put an end to Kiera so that I could move on with life and keep my family protected. After we finished dinner, I had to argue Saaleha down about just letting me clean the kitchen, and she just help Lil' Meen get ready for bed.

"As soon as he got out the tub, his little ass was out," Lee said when I came to sit next to her on the sofa. She scooted over to me and I instantly placed my arm around her shoulders. She leaned her left shoulder into my chest, and we got comfortable. "I miss times like this," she whispered. I think that was more so to herself, but it felt good hearing it.

"Me too." I kissed her forehead. "So, when are you taking this nut ass wig off?" I cracked.

"Don't do me! What, you don't like it?" Her cute ass pouted before her little elbow went into my side. I chuckled a little before I looked down at her hair and balled my face up. "Meenie!" she whined.

"I'm used to my natural Pocahontas. You don't do wigs. You got that shit these bitches pay for," was all I said before I pulled her wig off. She gasped really loud before she pushed me away from her. She stood there in front of me with two braids and her mouth wide open before tears welled in her eyes.

"Why would you do that!" she yelled before the tears finally fell out her eyes. Cry baby ass. I pulled her down so that she could straddle me. My hands automatically flew to her butt. "Meen, what—"

"Shut up," was all I said before I kissed her lips lightly. "You know I love you?" I whispered against her lips, forcing her to pull away. Her eyes lingered on mine before she looked away, then nodded her head. Placing my hand under I chin, I turned her to face me and kissed her lips again. "So, you know I won't stop at nothing to get you back? To get my family back."

"I know," was all she mumbled before she kissed me passionately. I didn't really care what her and True had. Saaleha was mine—always would be. And as long as she knew I wasn't going to stop until she came home, then we were cool. I knew True wasn't going to be so giving, but I was okay with going head to head with him. I'd go head to head over Saaleha. Instead of focusing on that though, I was going to pay special attention to my wife's body. All night.

Kiera Mitchell

The Meet Up

Omar sent me on a paid vacation to Cancun, and honey, I was living it up! I'd been down here for three days, by my lonesome, enjoying life. No man had ever sent me on a paid vacation anywhere; they always wanted to be under me. But ever since Omar started back working with Ronnie's uncle Rasta, he'd been getting paid. The money was rolling in, and baby, my life was great. But, speaking of Ronnie, he hadn't been answering my phone calls, with his ugly ass. We had a deal that I handle Ahmeen for him, and he'd keep my bank account laced for ten years. He cut his supply, five years early, and I needed my money. Stupid ass. Then on top of that, we were working on a plan to kill True too. Ronnie just wanted his uncle's respect. His uncle kept comparing him to Ahmeen and True; he had some deep issues with that. When I, on the other hand, just wanted my good old best friend's happiness taken away from her. I hated that bitch; always had and always would.

Speaking of my best friends, I hadn't talked to neither one of those bitches since they put Minah on to Rico. That was the fakest shit you could ever do to somebody. Like, how are you my best friend but putting bitches on my man? I swear those bitches were always lowkey jealous of me. They swore they were all that, but I knew the truth. Them bitches were frauds. Now Rico didn't even answer my calls. Some lady from his building told me he done moved out, and I didn't know none of his hangout spots. I tried to go to one of his offices, but his security told me that they had the right to kill me as soon as they saw me. Rico hated me that much, that he had a bitch on 'kill on sight.' He was too valuable. I knew Rico was falling in love with me, and I swear I blamed Omar's stupid ass. He knew he was my weak spot, and he knew what he was doing that day. He knew I wouldn't have turned him down for sex. I just wished I was being a little smarter and just told his ass no. Now my man was boo'd up with Aminah, and I was pissed. But it was okay; I was going to get his ass back and leave Aminah's ass sick.

I needed this vacation though, after the year I'd been having. As soon as I thought things were going great, something was taken away from me, or I had some shit to handle. My mom always told me life would catch up to me, but I didn't know what that meant. Shit, I lived and learned in every situation, do as I please, live how I want, and fuck other's opinion of me. That was what I told myself every single morning. My life was the card that was dealt for me, and I embraced it. Unlike most people who regretted things, I didn't regret a damn thing. I helped kill Ahmeen, and I'd do that shit all over. I ruined my best friend's life, and I'd do that shit all over too. It was life, it was my life, and I had no remorse or regret.

"Is this seat taken?" A woman's voice interrupted my thoughts. I was sitting out on the beach at this restaurant, waiting for my food. Looking up, I realized it was the bitch from the shop, who told Saaleha that True was her man. Now, I knew I didn't fuck with Lee like that, but I didn't play about her. Only I can do nut shit to her.

"Bitch, is you stupid?" I snapped, making her chuckle. She was pretty. She looked just like G Herbo's baby momma, Ari. Down to her body too. This bitch was bad, okurrt.

"Listen, I didn't come with harm. I just wanted to talk to you about something. Plus, I know you not stupid enough to try to fight me, in my city." She smirked as I looked around, not even noticing her security. Punk ass.

"What you want then?"

"Revenge." Her crazy ass smiled. "I know she's your *amiga* or whatever. But I also know you don't like her. I want revenge on Saaleha for taking my man."

"He told her you're just some bitch he fucks though, sis," I stated to her desperate ass. I hated desperate girls, like it's never that deep to be pressed over a man. I mean I am pressed over Rico, but not like this. Shawty actually looked hurt and sad over some dick that was never hers to begin with.

"What we had was an understanding, and little miss perfect came in and messed my shit up. I know all about you being the reason that Ahmeen is dead, so do you want me to tell her, or are you going to help me?" Her arrogant ass had the nerve to smirk. *How did she know all this?* I thought as we stared at each other.

"Help you how?"

"I want her dead." Dead? I never wanted Saaleha dead, ever. I cared about her too much, especially my baby, Lil' Meen. I couldn't take both of his parents away from him, I just couldn't. "It's either you help me, or I'll kill the both of you. Think about it," she said, shrugging before she stood, slipping her business card onto the table. Then she just walked away with her security.

For her to be a punk, she sent chills down my damn spine. And I feared nobody, ever. Flipping her business card over, I read her name about five times. *Kristina Gonzalez.* Her fake Ari looking ass. Shit, what the hell did you get yourself into now, Kiera? I guess I'd be calling her soon. I wasn't losing my life for nobody. Ever.

"You going to do what, Kiera?" Omar barked out. I had called him as soon as I got back into my hotel. I had to tell somebody about what Kristina offered. I knew he wasn't going to be with my choice, but what did he expect? I wasn't dying for nobody.

"I have to. This bitch might be a part of a mob or some shit. She said she'll kill me too, if I don't help her. Nigga, I am not dying," I snapped, taking a seat on the bed. Even though Omar used to be a heartless nigga, nowadays he's been thinking about his actions. All like 'we can't act off emotion no more', like boy bye. I don't know if its because he's been clean off them drugs, but I needed him to get back on that shit. I didn't need to be rational about shit right now, my life was on the line and I needed his support, just as every other time.

"You gotta be losing your mind, yo. You going to help somebody kill your best friend?" He paused. I sat there staring at the wall, as he breathed slowly into the phone. He probably was trying to wrap his mind around everything, but I just needed to know who side he was on. "Kiera, it's Saaleha we're talking about. I get you have problems with her and shit, but come on; she has a kid. A kid that you love and that we already took one parent away from."

Here he goes, making me think and shit, I thought as I sucked my teeth and rolled my eyes as if he could see me. He always been able to get into my head, get me to actually give a damn about things I do. It's crazy how only he had that ability. He could read, he understood me, and he could always see the good in me when nobody else can. Maybe this why I'll always be in love with him, because I personally think he was made for me. But right now, I needed him to just agree with what I want to do. I'm not trying to die.

"I know, Omar. But what you expect me to do? What are you going to do without me if I die? I have a life too, that I want to keep living." I sighed before laying back on the bed, closing my eyes allowing his breathing to smooth me. It was like I knew he wanted to be on a good track in his life for once, but he was selling guns with Rasta; he didn't want to be that damn good.

Letting out a deep breath, he spoke calmly but angry, "Seems like your mind is made up. I'm going to hit you up later. Enjoy the rest of your trip."

"Omar," was all I could get out before he hung up on me. He made valid points. I didn't want to do that to Lil' Meen, but it was either me or Saaleha, and I was picking me. Everyone was just going to have to deal with that. Lil' Meen would have Amber. He'd be alright.

Macion "Mack" Dupree
You with me or what?

Ever since I killed Cherelle, I'd been having nightmares of her. I was so happy that Reds didn't know about the nightmares. Shit, she'd already been acting iffy toward me. Well, I knew she was going through postpartum. She didn't want to claim it, because she always tried to be hard, but I knew my girl. Some days, she was good, but then some days, I'd watch her when she was around our daughter, and she'd just stare at her. She'd stare at Amaya as if something would happen to her. I overheard her the other day, crying while Amaya was crying. It fucked with me watching my girl like that. When I tried to talk to her about it, she'd brush it off, and we'd end up having sex. Saaleha tried talking to her because she went through the same thing, but it wasn't working. My girl was gone, and I didn't know when I was getting her back.

Anyway, I was laying here with my daughter, who was perfect, looking just like her mom, when Reds came in the room. She looked at us, and for the first time since Amaya's been born, she smiled. Taking out her phone, she snapped a couple pictures of us, then posted it on her Instagram.

"Y'all look so cute!" she said before she walked over to the bed and kissed me on the lips. She was so hot and cold nowadays, but I loved when she was in a good mood. I missed my girl. "I missed you today, babe."

"I missed you too. How was it being back at work?" I asked her as she walked out of the closet, pulling her nightgown over her head. She grabbed Amaya from my arms, kissing her on her face, then took her into her bedroom, before she came back into the bedroom, climbing into the bed. She laid on my chest. We hadn't cuddled at all this week.

"It was so rejuvenating to be back at the shop, to be doing hair again. It made me feel... I don't know. I felt like myself again." She sighed, while rubbing her hand across my stomach like she always did. She always said she loved the feel of my abs. "How was daddy and daughter day?"

"She shitted up her back, Reds. I almost left her like that." She started cracking up, making me laugh too. It felt good hearing her laugh, we've been co-existing around this jawn, so I was happy as hell right now. "It's not funny. That shit was nasty as hell too. I almost threw the whole baby away. I had to call my mom. I thought something was wrong with her shitty ass."

"Don't do my baby!" Reds yelled through laughter. This moment with her really felt good, we hadn't had nights like this since Cherelle died. I missed this Reds.

"I'm just saying. Something not right with your milk or something because it's no way a baby that little should be producing grown man shit." I smirked when Reds hit me on my stomach and laughed harder. "But, nah, that's daddy's baby. We chilled all day. I took her for a walk and shit like you told me too."

"Good. She needs to get fresh air sometimes. Thank you, baby." She leaned up and gave me a kiss on the lips. Looking into her eyes, I saw the love in her eyes, even though lately I didn't feel it, I saw it. "I love you, Macion," she said as she read me.

"I love you more," was all I said before inserting my tongue inside her mouth, which she kindly accepted. She climbed on top of me, straddling me, while I ran my hands up and down her sides. She leaned up and just stared at me, while I stared at her. "Are we good?"

"Why wouldn't we be?"

"Because ever since that day when Cherelle died, you've been distant, and I just need to know if we're good. That I'm not losing my girl." She stared down at me, while I held onto her waist. I never thought things would get like this between us, but honestly, what did I expect? I cheated on this girl our whole relationship, and it's like we got used to the toxic traits that we both had. Then with her hearing me say that I did love Cherelle, I knew that killed her. Never in the ten years we'd been together, had I ever loved another girl. Cherelle caught me at a time where I didn't think me and Amber would even get back together, because she was dating some corny ass rapper out New York. Nigga looked like SixNine. Spending time with Cherelle and getting to know her, made me grow love for her, but not how Amber thought.

"We're fine. We're always fine. I'm not going nowhere." Reds' voice broke my train of thought, as she leaned in and placed a soft kiss on my lips. "I promise, we in this for life," she whispered before we initiated in a deep, passionate kiss. Pulling away, she slid down my body until she got to her best friend, and she pulled him out.

"Handle it," was all I said before watching my dick disappear into her mouth. One thing about Reds, she could give some mean head. She was the champion of that shit. "Damn." She slurped, making it sloppy just how I like it before she paid special attention to the head. Gripping her hair, I was happy as hell she was wearing her natural hair because I was gripping that shit tight.

"Cum in my mouth," she murmured, and it was all she wrote. As I shot all my seeds down her throat, she swallowed them up before climbing on top of me. Pulling her nightgown up, she mounted on top of me. "Shiitttt," she moaned out.

"Why you so wet, yo?" I groaned at the feel of her. She smirked before she got on two feet and started bouncing on my dick. "Do that shit, Amber." She loved when I said her name. Her eyes would widen before the cutest smile would bless her face. Leaning forward, she stuck her tongue in my mouth, while I flipped her over onto her back.

"Mackkkk, I wanted to be in charge." She pouted, well tried to pout, but I was stroking her so deep, her mouth hung open instead. "Oh, I love you!"

"Tell me again." I sped my strokes up, trying to reach all of her. Her breath was caught in her throat while she scratched my back. "You don't hear me talking to you? Tell me again." I pulled away, just watching her as her hands ran up and down her body, and she reached for me again.

"I love you so much, Macion," she moaned out before opening her eyes. I leaned down and kissed her, not stopping my strokes. This was about to be a long night. I hoped our daughter slept through the night because once I was done with her mommy, she was going to have a sibling coming, real soon.

"How's your crazy ass baby momma?" Jay asked as he dapped me up, with Meen right behind him, walking inside of my barbershop. This nigga was just trotting around Philly like he didn't fake his death and shit.

"Nigga, you better stop playing with him about Reds." Meen chuckled before dapping me up too. I knew before I said I missed when it was us three, but I take that shit back. These niggas bothered me, always talking shit, with their yellow asses.

"Didn't they tell y'all?" I said, getting my clippers ready to cut Meen's hair. My boy needed a shape up bad. Whoever he was letting cut his shit in the DR, wasn't doing it right at all.

"Tell us what?" they asked in unison. Jay was sitting on the sofa in the shop eating chips like always, that's all he would eat.

"Light skin niggas not in style no more." I smirked when they both sucked their teeth. "Ah, y'all mad. It's not my fault these chicks nowadays like us chocolate niggas."

"Why your freak ass calling yourself chocolate though?" Jay asked with his face balled up, forcing a laugh out of Meen. Now it was my turn to suck my teeth and theirs to laugh.

"Man, I don't care what's not in style. Bitches love my light bright ass, no cap." Meen pulled on his beard.

"No cap, bro, but Saaleha don't fuck with your light bright ass," Jay joked, making me crack up. This nigga always talked shit, but he was right on the nose with that. Saaleha didn't mess with Meen at all, and she made it known every time he was around. Bro, wasn't giving up though, he was going hard for his wife.

"Now that's cap. She loves me."

"Anyway, have you talked to Rasta? Like, I don't need that nigga coming back trying to kill us and shit after you handled Ronnie." I knew that Rasta was all for Meen getting his revenge and shit, but at the end of the day, Ronnie was that nigga's nephew. Niggas didn't look past family shit. I knew I wouldn't.

"Rasta is the least of our worries. He's good. He moved on with his shit and put his youngest nephew in charge. It was a win for them both," he stated. But I had a feeling it was more, Meen kept us in shit, so I just knew it was more. "But who we need to watch our backs for is the Mexicans."

"Nigga, why? I thought we were cool with their asses," Jay spat. *I knew it,* I thought while I shook my head. Meen literally had no damn chill button, he always doing some dumb shit.

"We are, but Kristina is a Gonzalez; she's the daughter," Meen stated, making my and Jay's face ball up. I knew shawty looked familiar, a couple years back I had to make a shipment out in Mexico to the Gonzalez's and she was there. Shawty was bad as hell, but even I knew not to mess with a chick in the cartel. They be a different kind of slow, like mad different from regular hood chicks.

"Oh, nigga, that's your business." Jay shrugged before pulling out his phone. *This nigga,* I thought. We both stared at him, making him look back up. "Fuck y'all looking at me for? He the one who was dropping off dick to her crazy ass. Now watch, we about to be in some shit because she doesn't know what it means to be broken up with. So, if them Gonzalez niggas come after us, you, my nigga, gon' have to hand me in a one."

"Nigga, we the same size; nobody scared of you." Meen chuckled. Jay always wanted to fight somebody, but that was how we got through our shit. Fight then spark up. Jay calmed down a lot because he was a hot head while we were growing up, while Meen was a lowkey hot head, and I was the only laid back and chill one.

Reds always said we balanced each other out, and as I got older I realized we really did.

"Good, 'cause I'm dead ass. I'm going knock your ass out," Jay said, sitting up dumping the rest of his chips in his mouth, making me chuckle. *These two dickheads, yo.* We sat in the barbershop as I cut both of their heads, just talking like old times. Even though I had Amber shit on my mind and what we had going on at home, it was good to get it off my mind. I knew something was up with my girl, and I was going to get to the bottom of it. I just hoped she wasn't cheating on a nigga, because I was shooting first, asking questions later when it came to her.

Khyreema Jenkins
Everyone has a past, right?

Meeting Jayceon a year ago was the highlight of my life. He was so perfect, but our only problem was his hoe, Rhonda. I couldn't stand her, just like she couldn't stand me. Jay would jump back and forth between us two, and as much as I loved him, I wasn't settling for that. When I finally put my foot down, and said I was going to leave him, I ended up pregnant. I swear that be some type of punishment from God. As soon as you thought you were done with a nigga, you ended up pregnant. Unfortunately, I ended my baby's life because of my relationship with Jay, and he ended up hating me. I still remembered that night. He was so angry with me, he almost hit me; that's how mad he was. I was everything under the sun, literally. He called me everything but my name. I broke his heart that day. So, when I saw him at Paprika that day, I was beyond happy, and even happier that Kaylina was with me. Because if I was alone, he wouldn't have talked to me. He wouldn't have came over, and we wouldn't have rekindled.

It was crazy though. I hadn't been with a man since my daughter's father, Malcolm, who ruined my life completely. I met Malcolm when I was sixteen years old, and he was thirty years old, while I was living in Houston. Within two months of our relationship, he got me pregnant and started to show his true colors, which was abusive, verbally and physically. Not to mention, my mother hated the ground Malcolm walked on because she didn't understand why a man at his age would seduce a sixteen-year-old girl then impregnate her. While I was pregnant with Kaylina, I found out that Malcolm was married with a thirteen-year-old daughter at the time; three years younger than me. No lie, at sixteen, I didn't look my age. My body was very grown, but I was straightforward about my age to him. Malcolm, on the other hand, he wasn't so honest about his age. He told me he was twenty-one years old, and I believed him because he looked young. When I was about five months pregnant, I found out his age from his wife Danielle, who surprisingly was very nice to me.

Danielle told me when she found out about her husband's infidelities, she was furious, so furious that she followed him one day to the apartment I shared with Malcolm. She told me she waited for him to leave so that she could confront me. But when she saw me sporting a black eye, busted lip, and a five-month pregnant belly, she felt for me. She always said she knew off bat that I was just a little girl who got caught up in her husband's sick ways. Danielle helped me in every way that she could, especially after I had Kaylina. About three weeks after I gave birth to Kaylina, Malcolm beat me so bad because I wouldn't have sex with him before my six weeks were up. I didn't want to have another baby by him; I hated him. I called Danielle hysterical that night after he left me there to die. About two weeks following that, Danielle had a plane ticket for me to fly out to Philly to live. She had me set up in a beautiful four-bedroom home in Upper Darby, PA, that she got furnished for me. Ever since then, nine years ago, we stayed in contact, even spent every holiday and birthdays together. Danielle even divorced Malcolm and moved to LA to get her daughter away from his pedophile ass. It was easy moving on with life without him, but it was hard trusting a man.

Now, Jay didn't know the extent of my relationship with my daughter's father, because I didn't want to be judged. I didn't want anyone to know what I went through, because I didn't want anyone's pity. The other day, Danielle called me to tell me that Malcolm found her and told her he was coming for me. I didn't know why his ass was coming for me, but he was. So, her and her daughter Diamond, flew out here to stay with me. Meaning, I had to distance myself from Jay. Kaylina's ass had been going crazy. She kept asking about him, but me knowing my daughter, she'll run all my business in a heartbeat. So, I kept her away too.

I was laying on the sofa with Kay and Diamond, when my doorbell rang. I didn't even get a chance to get up, when the alarm went off. Diamond and I both stood when someone stopped the alarm, and Jayceon's stupid ass walked around the corner. I didn't know how this nigga got a key, let alone knew my damn security code!

"Why you acting like you seen a ghost?" his fine, ghetto ass had the nerve to ask, before his eyes flew to Diamond. "And who is you?" His cute face balled up, making me shake my head.

"Girl, he is finer than you said," Diamond mumbled, making me shake my head. She was right, Jayceon was such a beautiful man. I loved the freckles that went across his nose that he hated, I loved his facial hair that was sandy brown, and his low cut that was filled with waves. He was so tall, kind of lanky, but had muscles that I loved. His tattoos were my favorite art, I swear. I just loved everything about this man.

"Jay Jay!" Kaylina shouted, running up to him, as he held his arms open. As soon as she got close, he picked her up, and she wrapped her arms around him. The whole scene was so cute, even though I never asked him to play dad, he claimed her as his own. She had him wrapped around her little finger, and she knew it.

"What's up, Kay Kay? You being good?" He kissed her face before putting her down. She nodded her head before coming back to lay on the sofa. Diamond and I, on the other hand, were still standing and watching him. His fine ass strolled over to me before he pulled me into him and kissed me on the lips. "Have you been being good?"

Biting my bottom lip, I nodded my head before getting caught up in his eyes, forgetting Diamond was standing there. Clearing my throat, I stepped back a little befor speaking, "Babe, this Diamond, she's—"

"My big sister," Kaylina interrupted. My head snapped in her direction and her little grown ass had the nerve to shrug her shoulders. *I should smack her*, I thought before sucking my teeth. Jay's eyes widened before he looked between Diamond and I, then his eyes landed on Danielle as she walked out the kitchen.

"Her big sister? Khy, y'all look the same age." Jay said confusedly.

"Khy and I got caught up with an ain't shit nigga, which is why our daughters are sisters. I'm Danielle; you must be Jayceon. I heard so much about you." Danielle spoke up, and I was happy she did because I didn't know what to say. Jay nodded his head before pulling on his chin hair. I said chin hair because my boy just started growing a beard, and it was a little childish. But he was still fine as hell.

"Nice meeting y'all." He nodded before his eyes traveled to mine. "Come holla at me," was all he said before he walked away, heading to my bedroom. I took a deep sigh, while they started laughing. *I don't know why their laughing, Jayceon isn't wrapped tightly at all.*

"Girl, he got your ass all in check. And he is very daddyish; you better go, sis." Diamond stuck her tongue out, making me laugh.

"Seriously, because baby, he about to let you have it for keeping us a secret." Dani smirked before strutting away. She was right; he was about to curse me out. I stood there thinking that maybe if I went in there being sad, he'd take it easy on me.

"Khyreema!" he yelled from upstairs, making me suck my teeth. I walked slowly to the stairs, and he was standing at the top with his arms folded across his chest. "Don't play with me," he spoke before walking away. Pouting the rest of the way up the steps, I walked to my bedroom to find my fine ass boyfriend sitting at the edge of my bed, staring at me. He was looking good too, wearing a suit. Now, Jay didn't do suits, so to see him in this suit, it was doing some things to me. His ass was just beautiful.

"Stop drooling over me and get to talking," his cocky ass said. Rolling my eyes, I walked over to him and took a seat. I laid my head on his shoulder and sighed. He wrapped his arm around my shoulder and kissed my forehead. "You got me, Khy. No matter your story, I'm not going nowhere. I mean, unless you say you a recovering prostitute, then I might gotta bounce." I fell out laughing before play punching him in his arm. He played so much.

"You're so aggy."

"Nah, seriously though. Tell me your story, all of it," he said so genuinely, so I just talked. I told him everything, from the start to finish. I watched his eyes widen and his face ball up, but I didn't stop.

Different Sides Of The Game 2

I kept talking. I told him about the beatings, the lies, Danielle, and everything. I put it all out on the table for him. For the first time ever, I talked about my life, and it felt good; I felt relieved. He didn't say a word; he just listened to me, holding my hand, staring into my eyes. It was like he was reliving my pain with me, and honestly, it felt good just letting it all out.

"Wait, you said Diamond twenty-one? You're only twenty-four. What type freak shit was this nigga on?" Jay's face turned beet red, as he balled his fist up. He didn't pity me. He was angry that I had to go through this shit.

"I know. He lied about his age."

"What type female shit— you know what, I don't even care. As long as you good now, and he's a non-factor, we straight. You haven't seen him in nine years, right?" he asked, making me chuckle because his face was filled with disgust. "That shit not funny. I wanna kill this nigga."

"No, but he found them a couple weeks back, which is why they are here. He didn't threaten them or nothing, but he always told me that if I ever left him, he's going to kill me." I whispered the last part, just thinking about if Malcolm ever found me. Jay sucked his teeth, before he pulled me into his hard chest.

"As long as I'm in your life, that nigga will never lay a hand on you or baby girl head. I put that shit on my momma." He kissed my forehead. *Gangsta ass,* I smirked.

"I don't want to put you in my stuff, which is why I been distant, Jayceon," I said softly, before he kissed my plumped lips.

"I fucked niggas up for bumping me the wrong way. Picture what I would do to a nigga who fucks with mine?" He smirked, bringing a smile out of me. I swear I loved all that gangsta shit, what Summer Walker say in Girls Need Love? *I just need a thug.* "Dead ass though, I got you. Don't worry about that nigga at all. Your shit is my shit."

"I'm kind of happy I have you in my life now, with your yellow ass." I winked at him, making him playfully push me off him.

"My dick big as shit though." He smirked, making my mouth drop 'cause, baby, he wasn't lying. That thing was dangerous, and I was dangerously in love with that shit too.

"Wait, Jay. How the freak you get a key to my house?" I asked as I remembered him just walking into my shit like he owned it.

"Got a key made." He shrugged his shoulders like that was cool or something. I shook my head because I didn't know what I was going to do with him. He thought that was justifiable. "So, what we going to do about this interior designing? I mean, you did just graduate. We need to get that shit popping," he said.

Back in May, I graduated from college, finally, in the major of interior design. That was the happiest day of my life, and even though Jay and I weren't speaking, he still came to show me love. Before our whole baby fiasco, I told him that I wanted to open my own interior design business, called Styled by Kaylina, named after my daughter. He always said he was going to buy my building for me, but when we stopped messing with each other, that dream left right with him.

"Well, I've been looking at buildings, trying to get a feel of them. I just don't know what area I want to open it up at, maybe Downtown? I'm not sure." I shrugged.

"Downtown would be nice, just let me know. You know I'm going to foot whatever bill." See, I loved him. I always had to do things on my own with being a single mother, that when he came around, I didn't know what it was like to have a man take care of me. He always paid for things and would air me out if I attempted to take out my wallet. A couple times, I paid for dinner before he got the chance too, and honey, he cursed out every server. I didn't care either because it was the least I could do.

"So, are you still selling drugs or?" I asked, making him fake gasp and grab his chest dramatically. Since I'd known him, I knew he had money, and since he kept me in the dim about his business life, I just assumed that he was a drug dealer just like Ahmeen and Mack.

"Wow, that's what you think of me?" He shook his head, making me laugh. "I haven't sold drugs since I was a pup, ma. I'm in arms dealings. But you know I do own a few clubs in different states. And I do real estate."

"Do you run those with your gang?" I asked, making him fall out laughing.

"Gang? I'm a grown ass man, Khyreema," he said, making me chuckle. "We own about two clubs together, but me and Meen the only ones in real estate. Mack own a few barber shops and a strip club out Miami. We trying to get him into real estate with us," he said.

"Y'all really legit men. I would've never known." When Saaleha would say that her and Meen were in real estate before he faked his death, I didn't believe her. Well, I believed she might've been, but a hood nigga? Child, no.

"What you mean? We went to college, man." He laughed. "We graduated and everything. I was valedictorian."

"You dead ass?" I asked, shocked. Why didn't I know this about his ass?

"Naw, I was valedictorian in high school though, no cap." *He annoys me,* I sucked my teeth making him chuckle. "You were about to OD. I wish I went to college though."

"You still have time to."

"Ma, I'm already a multi-millionaire. I'm straight." He winked at me before pulling me closer to him. He kissed my lips a few times before we decided to go back downstairs. I didn't know what I was going to do if Malcolm found me, but I was happy as hell I wouldn't have to go through it alone. It was nice to have a man around, especially one like Jayceon's fine ass.

Amber "Reds" Wright

Hood Sophisticated

I never thought being a mom would be this amazing. I loved my daughter with all of me, she was perfect. She had Mack's perfect chocolate skin tone, with my face. She was mommy's baby. Even though my daughter was perfect, Mack and I wasn't. Ever since that day Cherelle called herself kidnapping me and Mack telling me he had love for her ass, things hadn't been the same. Telling me that you had love for another bitch, made me feel as if he was downplaying the fact that he did love her. Honestly, that shit broke my damn heart. I never thought that my man would ever fall in love with someone else. Then on top of that, he had nightmares of her every night. He didn't think I knew, but he would say her name in his sleep, and would be sweating. He even said that he loved her. That alone messed with me. It broke me in ways that he didn't even know. I had even been suffering from postpartum. But I wasn't no weak bitch. I wasn't trying to claim it, even though I knew I was suffering with it.

No matter what Macion did, it didn't faze me. I wasn't moved by the flowers, the loving, or nothing. I told him that I wasn't leaving him, but at this moment, mentally, I wasn't there. I still had sex with him of course; that dick was too bomb to be giving up. It was like I was wishy washy with him. Some days I wanted to be around him; I wanted to be under him. Then some days, I didn't want nothing to do with him. It wasn't fair to him, but him cheating on me for ten years with multiple bitches wasn't fair to me. A part of me hated him for making me a weak bitch. I hated that I allowed him to think it was okay to cheat on me. For him to even have a bitch think she was pregnant by him, killed me. I took him back each time since I was fifteen, and I was so angry at myself for that.

Anyway, I was over True's house with Saaleha. Mack had our daughter for the night. Even though I was scared of him being alone with her, Saaleha talked me into it. Talking about some 'let him be a dad', as if she wasn't scared back then about leaving Lil' Meen with Ahmeen's crazy ass.

"I can't believe I let you talk me into leaving my baby with Macion's ass," I said as we sat in the living room. Saaleha sucked her teeth before flagging me.

"Girl, bye. He's her father." She rolled her eyes while I stuck my middle finger up at her.

"Pick a side and stay there," I mumbled, making her fall out laughing. She always picked Mack's side, unless he did some fuck boy shit. Then she was team Reds.

"I'm hungry. I want some breakfast from June's." Lee dramatically laid on my shoulder, rubbing her stomach.

"Yo, we used to go there every morning before school. Kiera used to be like 'I don't care if we late, I need to eat!'" I said, making us laugh. I missed being in high school, life was hard but so easy. "I miss Overbrook, man."

We continued talking about the old days, until True's friend, Montez walked in. Honey baby, his ass was fine with a capital F. Y'all know I have a thing for chocolate niggas, but his light skin ass was just gorgeous. He was everything. He looked exactly like Chris Brown's fine ass. He was a thick, tall nigga. Like not fat, but thick, built of muscles. Child, I think I was in love. He was wearing a white Polo tee with some Adidas joggers. His print, baby, that print was all the way there. I'd seen him a few times, but now I was really seeing him.

"Stop staring at him, hoe," Saaleha whispered, interrupting my sexual thoughts. I looked over at her, and she wore a smug grin before chuckling. Listen, I've been so deep and dumb in love, I only be seeing my man. I have never thought another man was this fine, since like ever.

"Girl, his ass is fine," I mumbled, before he showcased his pearly whites as if he heard me. They were so perfect, and so white. I loved

Different Sides Of The Game 2

a nice ass smile on a man, that made them sexier, because that meant they took care of themselves. I hated a man who didn't believe in going to the dentist or doctors, that was beyond me.

"How you doing, Amber?" Montez's deep voice boomed through the living room, making my panties wetter than they already were. I looked up at him, finally noticing that he was standing dead in front of me. He licked his lips before he gave me the cutest smile.

Clearing my throat, I stuttered, "I-I'm good, how about you?" *Nice going, idiot*, stuttering and shit. He smirked before looking at Saaleha, making me look at her too. Her stupid self was just staring at us with her mouth open.

"I'm straight, you look good." Montez bit his bottom lip, before he took a seat next to me. He had me tripping, I had to look down at what I was wearing because last time I checked, I looked a mess. I was wearing a pair of PINK tights, a t-shirt, and some damn Vans. My hair was up in a messy bun, and I wasn't wearing any makeup. I mean at least my lash extensions were popping. "I like girls chilling, not all done up," he whispered in my ear, as if he read my mind.

"Lee, come upstairs with me real fast." True's voice interrupted me and Montez's stare down.

"Why do you need me to come upstairs with you, True?" Saaleha's face balled up, making me laugh. She was so clueless. I swear I loved my good sis, with her slow ass.

"Girl, bring your ass," True yelled, making her suck her teeth, then start pouting. "Saaleha!"

"Okay, damn." She rolled her eyes, before getting up and tending to her man, who swore he was slick. After Saaleha told me she'd be back, she stomped her way to the stairs. "Your ass probably doesn't even want anything!" She yelled as she stomped up the stairs, like the big baby she was.

"She's so slow." I chuckled. My eyes traveled back to Montez, who's eyes were examining me as if he wanted to take my mind and soul. For some reason, I instantly became nervous. Like, I, Amber, was nervous. I was never nervous around nobody, except Macion. This was beyond me.

"You want to go grab something to eat? I didn't eat all day," Montez suggested. I sat there thinking it over because I really did want to go with him. Shoot, he could've asked me to go to a hotel, and I would've gone with him! After I agreed to go, I sent Lee a text to let her know that I was going with Tez to grab something to eat. Leaving out, we walked to his Tesla Model S, and this man, and I say *man*, held the door open for me. Like he helped me into the car. Mack's annoying ass would never. When I was pregnant, yeah, but that was only for those nine months, with his rude ass.

As soon as I got in the car, my phone went off indicating I had a text, I was praying to God that it wasn't Macion. I didn't feel like lying, nor did I feel like feeling bad. For once, I wanted to do what he done to me, and feel what he felt when he met Cherelle, or any bitch he stepped out on me with. Looking down at my phone, I fell out laughing because it was nobody but Saaleha.

Bestie Boo: *DINNERRRR? *Soulja Boy voice* hoe you not slick. I could've cooked something.*

Me: *Can I live? Damn! It's just dinner, byeeeeee!*

"Where you want to go?" Tez's voice broke my focus. Looking over to him, I smiled softly. *Damn, he fine,* I thought as I stared at him.

"It's this place called *Tortilla Press Cantina*, it's in Cherry Hill. We can go there," I suggested because that was me and Saaleha's spot, and plus Macion didn't know anything about it. He agreed with me and we headed over there. About twenty minutes later, we pulled up at the restaurant and he parked, came around, and helped me out the car. He was either a gentleman, or he was trying too damn hard. But either way, I was feeling it. Happy that it wasn't crowded, we sat ourselves and was greeted and ordered immediately.

"Why you picked this place?" he asked once the server left. Shrugging my shoulders, I looked around the restaurant, just thinking about how many times Saaleha and I came here whenever shit was going bad. This place was like our peace away from the world. Plus, their margaritas and tacos were everything.

"I don't know. Saaleha and I found out about this place when we turned twenty-one, and it just became our spot away from life." I guess he liked my answer because he smiled. Boy, he was fine with his light bright ass.

"So, tell me something about you?"

"Well, I'm a new mom. I have the most amazing baby girl. Her name Amaya. Saaleha and I are partners, we own the glam shop together. I graduated college in a major of finance, and I'm working on opening my own financial firm. I think it's been long enough. I need to stop playing," I expressed. Opening my own financial firm has always been my dream, but being the girlfriend of Macion selfish ass put a pause on that. I always put him and his dreams before my own, he didn't think I needed to open one. He thought I should be content with the way I was living, he thought I cared about the foreign cars, designer clothes, and fancy living. Yeah, it was nice, but it's nothing wrong with expanding yourself or your brand.

"Well, it's never too late. I own an accounting firm, so I could help you with that. If you want my help," he offered. *Finally, somebody who was into the shit I was into, outside of Saaleha,* I smiled staring at this man God hand picked himself. "Are you originally from Philly?"

"Yup, West Philly born and raised. You not from here?"

"Nah, I'm from Opa Locka, but I live in New York now. You ever been to Opa Locka?"

"No, but I want to go because that's where the City Girls from," I said, making him laugh. "If you live in New York, why you always in Philly?"

"Business purposes; trust me, I barely like y'all cocky motherfuckas. Especially that nigga Meek—"

"Uh no! Don't do Meek. I don't play about him, I'm a big fan and Philly stands together when it comes to him," I interrupted him, making his hands go up in a surrendering way, he let out the cutest chuckle, making me smile my damn self. I wasn't playing either, Philly will go to war over Meek Mill fine ass.

"My bad, lil' baby. You better go that hard for me too." The smirk he gave me had me like *'yes daddy'*. I was ready for whatever ride he was going to take me on. It was my time to have fun, Mack would be fine. 'Cause baby, this boy right here was the devil, I could tell.

Forgive me Lord, for I have sinned!

Saaleha Santana

Gotta Tell Him the Truth

Best Red: *Girl, I think I'm in love with Tez. We've been on three dates so far, he is just sooooo perfect!*

Me: *I'm snitching, hoe!*

Best Red: *And I'ma whoop that ass!*

I chuckled at Reds' last message, before placing the phone back down. Her hot in the box ass was going to get caught up. I didn't blame her though, because Montez was definitely a sight to see. Plus, I knew she never really fully gotten over everything Macion put her through. I just wanted and needed her to be careful, cheating on Mack with Montez is like playing with fire. I just hope it doesn't burn down. Anyway, I was lying in bed when I should've been getting dress. True wanted to do dinner tonight, but honestly, I couldn't get me cheating on him out of my head. I cheated on his perfect ass, with Ahmeen's dumb ass. Twice! Well, like ten because I lost count of how many rounds we went in those two nights. I was so angry with myself, y'all don't understand. I done messed up with a good man, even though he had his shit with him; he was a good man. All because my baby daddy, who was still my husband, faked his death. I wished I could just punch Meen in his face, but I couldn't even blame him. I wanted to have sex with him just as much as he wanted to have sex with me. What was I going to do? I couldn't believe myself.

Breaking my thoughts, True's fine ass walked into his bedroom, looking scrumptious. He was wearing some Mike Amiri jeans, with a Fendi shirt on that was snug on his muscles. Honey, my man was so fine. His cute face balled up when he noticed I was still lying in bed.

"Babe, I thought I told you to be dressed when I got here," he said, walking over to the bed. My eyes followed his movements as he sat down on the bed. "What's wrong?"

Shrugging my shoulders, I sighed. "I don't feel too good." It wasn't a lie, I didn't feel good. Lately, my stomach had been bothering me, and I'd been having major headaches. I thought I'd just been stressed.

"We can just chill here then, babe, what you want to eat?"

"Pizza, buffalo chicken fries, and cake." I smiled when his eyes widened. "I'm PMSing, don't do me." Chuckling he nodded before going into his closet. He stripped out of his clothes, then called the pizza store for us. Once our food came, we laid in his bed watching *Claws*, on *Hulu*. He hated this show, but I loved it, okay.

"You really be having me watching anything," he inquired, making me laugh. Leaning back into his chest, I shrugged.

"It's a good show. Don't be a hater." I pouted but smiled when he kissed my cheek. I couldn't fathom why I stepped out on him. I didn't care if Ahmeen was my husband; to True I was still a widow. I was his girl, nobody else's. Maybe I could kill Meen and then move on with life. No, I'm just playing. I loved his yellow ass too much, and I loved my son more. *Ugh, this is stressful*, I thought to myself.

"I really could get used to this, being cuddled up with you for the rest of my life and shit. I'm happy I met you, and I'm happy that you decided to give me another chance." He paused before he sat up, forcing me to lean up too. Why was he pouring his heart out to me? *I am a hoe, True. You don't want me*, I thought to myself. My eyes stayed on him, while he walked into his closet, then came out with a red Cartier box. *Oh, hell naw*, I yelled in my head.

"W-what's that?" I stuttered, praying it was some earrings. *Please be earrings! Please be earrings!* I screamed in my head. Chuckling, he walked over to me, grabbing my hand, pulling me to the end of the bed, while he kneeled in front of me.

"When you see me kneel like Kaepernick, call a reverend, 'cause I got a milli in the stash for a wedding. If you ready let me know, 'cause it's whatever," he rapped Meek Mill's song '24/7'. My mouth dropped open when he opened the box, because the ring was just that beautiful. Bigger than the one Meen got me. "It might be too soon being as though my wife passed, but in my opinion this feels right to me. They say people come in your life at the right time, for all the right reasons. Yours was to help me cope with the death of Monica, to help me fall in love again, and know that it's okay to love again. Thank you for that. You fit me perfectly, Lee. I love you and Lil' Meen, and I want y'all in my life forever, with more babies. So, baby, do me the honor and become my wife."

Now, why he had to do this to me. Tears fell from my eyes, while I thought about how I was about to break his heart. He stared at me with so much anticipation. Looking to the ceiling, I took a deep breath. "Baby, I would love to become your wife." I paused looking down at him, while the cutest smile graced his face. *Damn.* "But I can't."

"What you mean you can't? Lee, I—"

"Ahmeen is alive," I interrupted. His eyes widened before he got up from the kneeling position and sat next to me. "So, I'm technically still married to him."

"What you mean he's alive? How you know?" He stared at me with his jaws tight. He was angry, and I didn't blame him. He wanted to get married, shit so did I, but with Meen back now; it complicated things more.

"Well, when my dad had called me to DR that time, I went and got a shocker. That's when I found out; that was why when I returned home, I was acting weird. Because I didn't know how to tell you. I was scared. Plus, I was still in disbelief that all this time he was alive." I paused. "But it's more. I fucked up big time."

"How you—" He paused before he stood up and faced me. "You fucked him? Didn't you?" *Now why he had to ask me like that? I* thought. I didn't know what to say, as I stared at the man that I was falling in love with. "Huh, Lee? Did you fuck him?"

"It was a mistake, True. I swear, a vulnerable moment. I took Ahmeen Jr. to go see him that week I went to DR—"

"And you took my son with you?" he interrupted me, breaking my heart. He loved Lil' Meen so much. I was glad I only brought up the one time, because if he knew I did it twice, baby, he'd probably kill me. Standing up, I wrapped my arms around his waist. He tried to push me off, but I wouldn't let go. I could not lose him, I didn't want to lose him. I loved him to much.

"He wanted to see him. I can't deny him of his son, True," I said, causing him to shake his head. He tried to push me off him again, but I tightened my grip.

"Move" he said calmly. I shook my head no, he angrily chuckled before grabbing my arms and yelling, "Move, Saaleha!"

"No, I'm not moving! We are going to talk! You're not leaving me, we're not breaking up, we're going to get married. Baby, don't do this. Talk to me," I begged him. It was this moment that I realized that I was in love with him. I was madly in love with True.

"What's there to talk about? You hid the fact that this nigga was still alive. Then you took Lil' Meen to go see him without even telling me, and somehow your hoe ass ended up on his dick! Maybe you and Kiera are the same," he spat coldly, while I stared at him. His heart was broken, and it was all my fault.

"Don't leave me." I spoke so low, scared of his response, so scared to lose him. "Please don't leave me." I spoke again, cuffing his face. He stared down at me, shaking his head.

"You still love that nigga?" he asked. I didn't know what to say, because I did still love him, but not the way he thought. I must've taken too long to respond because he chuckled. "I should've known that you weren't over this nigga. Damn, that's my fault though." He picked me up to move me before he walked away. I grabbed the back of his shirt before jumping in front of him. "Saaleha, move!" he yelled, causing me to jump. His brown skin was almost red, and his veins in his arms were popping out and his jaw kept twitching.

"No! I'm not moving! I do love him, but I am not in love with him! I'm in love with you! I made a mistake, and I'll spend every day of my life making it up to you, but I'm not letting you leave me, True! Please don't leave me," I begged him with tears falling rapidly. He just stared at me. "Say something!" I yelled, and he shook his head. I knew that he still loved his wife, I accepted that, why couldn't he accept this?

"I want you gone when I get back," was all he said before he moved to walk out the door. My heart started beating rapidly, and the room started spinning before I felt a sharp pain shoot through my body. All I remembered was screaming True's name, before I passed out, again.

True Taylor

Momma's Baby, Daddy Maybe?

No chick, and I mean no chick, had broken my heart the way Saaleha just had. Hearing her tell me that she fucked her ex, killed me, especially since I just got down on my knee and proposed to her ass. I wasn't mad when she said Ahmeen was still alive. I was mad because her naïve ass fucked him. I swear Saaleha had to be the most naïve person I've ever met. I hated that she always wanted to see the good in situations, like if Monica would've faked her death than came back, she wouldn't exist to me. This nigga left her in pain for five years, and now he back and she's opening legs? Nah, that shit is beyond me. Then on top of all that she had the nerve to pass out, making me scared. She always passed out. I hated that she was that overdramatic, but this time she had a reason. After I called her parents and Reds to the hospital, they ended up bringing Meen. That shit pissed me off. What the fuck was he there for?

"What's good, True?" Meen smirked, trying to give me a handshake. Chuckling, I smacked his hand out of my way. "Don't disrespect me, yo!"

"Or what? Nigga, you bleed the same blood as me. I put you on, nigga. Don't bite the hand that fed you!" I barked, stepping into his face. "So, what's good, lil' nigga?"

"Can y'all chill? We here for Lee, not for who dick bigger. Back up, Meen." Reds stepped in between us, pushing us apart. "Ahmeen!"

"On bro, you might want to listen to her. 'Cause how I'm feeling right now, I might just knock you the fuck out." I spoke calmly, making Reds suck her teeth.

"True, please!" she yelled. "Meen, leave! He needs to go in there; she just woke up."

"Nah, I need to go in there. She my wife!" his bitch ass yelled, and that was it for me. Punching him dead in his shit, he stumbled back, wiping the blood off his lip. He ran toward me, and we started fighting until we were being pulled away from each other. Montez had his arms wrapped around me, and Reds and Mack were holding onto Meen, while Jay stood there, eating chips, shaking his head.

"Y'all need to stop it!" Saaleha's mom, Saleemah, yelled out.

"He hit me first," Meen's childish ass said, making me chuckle. *She picking this nigga over me?* I thought to myself as I stood there ready to take his head off.

"Boy, shut up. Sounding like a little ass boy instead of a grown ass man. Take your ass on while True go in and check on her. She's asking for him, not you!" Saleemah snapped, pushing Meen with her toward the elevators while Mack and Jay followed, leaving me alone with Montez and Reds, who was just staring at each other. These two.

"What's up, Reds?" Tez smirked, making her blush.

"Hi, Montez," she flirted back, making me shake my head. Her little ass was bold, as if her nigga wasn't just up here.

"Just remember your nigga here," was all I said to Reds, making her nod her head quickly. I didn't need for Mack and Tez getting into anything over Reds because she wants to be cheating. I mean birds that flock together do thot together. I walked into Saaleha's room, who was sitting up, trying to get out of bed, probably because she heard all the commotion. She stopped when she saw me and just stared at me. She was so beautiful, as her grey eyes stared into my soul, and her hair was pulled into a loose ponytail. She was perfect. *Why did she have to go do some nut shit?* I asked myself. Shaking my head, I walked over to her and helped her back into the bed before I took a seat next to it.

"What happened to your face?" Her soft voice flowed through my body, making me shake my head. She had me on some soft shit.

"Your husband got out of line, so..." I trailed off before shrugging my shoulders. She took a deep breath before reaching for my hand, but I didn't budge. "So, look, I know I don't have to question you on this, because you just found out he was alive recently. But I'm going to still ask..." I paused. "You're three and a half months pregnant, which explains a lot. Are you sure that this baby you are carrying is mine before I get excited about that?"

"I'm three months? I would've known. I know my body—"

"Well clearly you don't. So, again is that my baby?" I asked, making her suck her teeth. I didn't know what her attitude was about. She was the one who fucked a nigga on me.

"If I'm three and a half months pregnant, yes, this is your baby!"

"So that means you fucked him while my seed is in there," I said more so to myself. I could really kill her right now. That's some shit you just don't do, you don't give your nigga pussy away, especially while you're pregnant with his seed.

"I didn't know, True. I'm—" She stopped when I held my hand up. I didn't want to hear shit she had to say. The fact of the matter was that she fucked a nigga while my seed was inside of her, which was the most disrespectful thing she could've ever done.

"Whatever. Listen, don't call me unless it's about the baby. I want to know about all doctors' appointments and shit like that."

"True. Please."

"Saaleha, don't call me unless it's about the baby," was all I said before I left out the room. I heard her calling my name, and as much as I wanted to go back, I couldn't. Saaleha fucked up this time, and I was not sure if it was any coming back from this one.

First Doctors' Appointment

I hadn't spoken to Saaleha since we found out she was pregnant. I ignored all her apologizing text messages and everything. I didn't have anything to say to her honestly. I still couldn't believe she fucked Meen. I didn't care about no vulnerable moment. As my chick, you shouldn't have no vulnerable moments. Then on top of that, I had to be around this nigga because of Lil' Meen. Everybody tried to get me to understand her point of view, as if she didn't cheat on me. It wasn't justifiable; she cheated on me. Then it was like I couldn't even blame her, because I knew if it was Monica, I'd probably do the same thing. But I also knew Monica would never pull no corny shit like faking her death, so Saaleha wouldn't have even been a factor if she never got sick.

I had just got to Saaleha's doctors' appointment, and as happy as I was that we were having a baby, I was pissed off that we weren't even speaking. Walking inside, I spotted her almost immediately because that was how strong our energy was. Plus, she was the prettiest girl in the room. She sat in the chair, engrossed in her phone. Her stomach was still flat, which was why we didn't even know she was pregnant. It was still summer, so she wore a pair of ripped jeans, probably from Fashion Nova because she was obsessed with their jeans. She had a crop top on, showing off her stomach, and her latest tattoo of an elephant on her shoulder. Her hair was up in a messy bun, and she didn't have on any makeup. As I sat there and admired her, I noticed half of the niggas in here was admiring her ass too, as if they weren't in here with their baby moms. She must have finally felt me because she looked up at me, rolling her eyes and looking back into her phone.

"Saaleha Santana." The nurse called her name before I even got to sit down. Saaleha stood up immediately, walking past me, not even acknowledging me. Chuckling lightly, I shook my head and followed behind her. "You can take everything off and slip this gown on. Dr. Marsh will be right with you," the nurse said to Saaleha before her eyes traveled to mine, and she bit her bottom lip.

"Bitch, he doesn't want you. You not his type, now get out," Lee barked, causing the girl to put her head down and walk out. She was right, she wasn't my type. Shit, only Saaleha was my type. "No respect having ass."

"You didn't have to be mean; she just was looking." I smirked when she sucked her teeth. She turned to face me with her arms folded, as she looked me up and down. "What?"

"You get out too so I can change," she had the audacity to say. Sucking my teeth, I sat in the chair and pulled out my phone. I didn't know why she was the one with the attitude; she cheated on me.

Once she noticed I wasn't moving, she huffed and puffed before unbuttoning her jeans. I tried to act like I was into my phone, but, how could I? Her body was out of this world, I wasn't missing out on seeing it. She tugged her jeans down, and she was wearing my favorite color gray laced panties. Turning her back toward me, she took her top off and she didn't have a bra on. Standing up, I walked over to her and pulled her into me.

"True," she spoke softly, but I turned her around, silencing her with a kiss. Picking her up, I placed her on the table, while attacking her neck. Her hands flew to my sweat pants and she pulled my dick out. Pulling her panties to the side, I helped her guide me inside of her.

"Damn," we both moaned out. I missed the feel of her, the way she fit me like a glove, then on top of that, she was soaking wet. They weren't lying when they said pregnant pussy was the best pussy. I'd fuck around and keep her pregnant. *Damn, we not together anymore.*

"Baby, I'm going to cum." Her soft moans broke my train of thought. I leaned up and looked her in the eyes. I saw all the love she had for me in them. I saw that she was sorry, but that wasn't enough. Men could cheat and not have no emotional attachment to another girl, and still be madly in love with his chick. But when a woman cheated, it was emotionally, mentally, and physically. I knew that Meen held parts of that because, at the end of the day, he was her first everything. He was still her *husband.*

"Me too. Cum on my dick, Lee." I groaned as I picked up my pace. Her nails sunk into my back deeper, and I bit her shoulder so that I wouldn't moan out like a bitch. Her body shook, and it felt like an ocean erupted onto my dick, while I shot my seeds deep inside of her. We sat there for a little before I pulled out of her. Her eyes stayed on me while I went inside of her bag and pulled out some wipes. Walking over to her, I wiped her off before helping her into the gown and back onto the table.

"True, I—"

"Can I come in now?" Lee was interrupted by her doctor as she walked in the door. "You and Amber have to do better," she said, making Lee and I laugh.

"Hi, Dr. Marsh. How are you?" Saaleha spoke through a smile.

"I'm great. It seems like we're always pregnant at the same time! I'm four months." Dr. Marsh smiled before showcasing her small stomach. The two of them talked the whole appointment. When I heard my baby's heartbeat, I swear a nigga cried. Saaleha held my hand the entire time, while we both cried like some big babies. It was crazy 'cause at that moment, my love for Lee deepened. She was about to give me my first child ever. This shit was big to me.

Walking out of the doctors' office, I walked Lee over to her car. Before she got in the car, I stopped her and pulled her into a hug. We stood there for a little, just hugging. I felt her heartbeat pick up as if she was nervous.

"Thank you, Saa."

"You don't have to thank me. We did this together," she said softly as she pulled away. She already knew what I was thanking her for. I stared in her eyes while she stared into mine. Sighing deeply, she spoke again. "I'm really sorry, True. And I—"

"Just give me time, that's all I ask. I need time to deal with the fact that you fucked your ex," I spat, not trying to sound cold, but every time I thought about it, it pissed me off. Her eyes watered before she nodded and pulled away from me. "Saaleha," I started before she shook her head and got into her car, leaving me there staring at her while she pulled off.

I didn't know what we were going to do, but we just needed to focus on our baby. We could deal with the extra shit later.

Amber "Reds" Wright

You feel the vibe, it's contagious.

"Montez, stop!" I chuckled trying to run from him but was to slow because he picked me up. We were at Sky Zone and I swear I haven't had this much fun in forever. I haven't seen him in a week because I was been busy with mom life, working, and trying to open my financial firm. He has been great help too, I had eventually stopped going to Macion about it, and started going to Montez. He's been going places with me downtown to check out buildings, helping me with my business plan, and everything. I truly appreciated him.

"Aight, come on you ready to go?" He placed me back on my feet before placing a kiss on my cheek. Nodding my head, I finished putting my shoes on and then we headed out. He always took me on cute dates and paid me so much attention. Attention that Macion didn't give me. "What you want to do now?"

"How about we go back to your place, and you cook me some dinner?" I smiled brightly, forcing a laugh out of him. I just wanted to be around him, it was like his vibe was contagious. He made me happy.

"You know I live in New York, lil baby. You sure you can go?" He cracked making me roll my eyes. Flagging him, I walked towards his car, I was grown. Plus, Saaleha and Khyreema had all the kids tonight because Mack, Jay, and Meen were away on business. So, I was in the clear, so it was act up time. Montez got in the car and stared at me with a smug grin.

"What?"

"Don't walk away from me ever again, Amber. I'm not no nut ass nigga." He demanded making me roll my eyes. But really in my head I was like 'okay daddy'. To say face, I sucked my teeth before flagging him.

"Whatever bro, we're going to your house or what?" I asked as he stared at me for a little, before nodding his head. He started the car up and drove off. Since we went to the Sky Zone in New Jersey we were about a good two hours away from his house. So, I started to get comfortable, so I can go to sleep.

"Oh, naw baby. You not going to sleep. You better get up, sing to a nigga, talk to a nigga or something." He snapped making me laugh, he so stupid.

"Sing to you? Don't play with me, I will hit that high note."

"You know what? Just talk to me, that's better. I don't got time for you breaking my ears." He sucked his teeth as if I really was bothering him. Sticking my middle finger up, I took my sneakers off and put it on his dashboard. "You real comfortable, didn't your mom ever tell you don't put your feet on people shit."

"Only parent I ever had was Saaleha's mom, and we were allowed to put our feet on her shit." I stuck my tongue out making him chuckle.

"What happen with your peoples?" I knew he was going to ask, because I never brought up my family. Shit, they didn't even exist to me. Shrugging my shoulders, I looked out of the window, I felt myself feeling weak. My family was a touchy topic because that's all I ever wanted.

"Uh, my dad denied me because he didn't want kids, and my mom focused so hard on trying to prove to him that I was his, she never really was around. She left me at Saaleha's house one night when I was sixteen, and I haven't seen her or my dad since. She does send me money in a card every year for my birthday, but that's about it. Never no return address, never a 'I miss you', just always money and a message that says, 'I'll always love you.' So, I don't really have a biological family, just an add-on family." I wiped the tears that fell down my eyes, forcing Montez to grip my thigh.

"Damn, shawty. I didn't mean to make you cry,"

"It's fine, that's why I always stayed with Macion. He's basically all I know, plus he gave me a family. I want my daughter to have a family that I didn't have. Family is really important to me." I sighed.

"I get it, trust me I do. Even though I grew up with both my parents, and the instilled in me that family was important. But what I am going to say, and you don't have to respond. Just don't take offense." He paused. He looked over at me and I nodded my head, I mean I wasn't sure if I was going to be okay with what he was about to say. But I'll try. "You're an amazing woman, since I've known you. I get that when niggas young, we fuck up. Shit, I fucked up with my ex girl and now she married with two beautiful kids. Us men have the tendency of not knowing what we got when we have it until it's gone. But I also have two little sisters, and I always tell them to always respect themselves. I always make sure that though know that a nigga only going to do what you allow them to do. And as I get to know you, I know you're far from weak, but you're weak for him. He knows that you're weak for him too, so that's why he always did what he did because he knew that you weren't going to leave him, he—"

"That's not true, I left him multiple times." I interrupted him, I didn't like the fact that he was telling me about myself like this. He chuckled lightly before licking his perfect pink lips.

"You went back every time." He coolly replied as if he didn't just play the shit out of me. "Look, I can't tell you what you're worth if you don't believe it. I try to show you every chance I get when I'm with you, but you gotta know your worth too." He simply shrugged before cutting the music up, as if the conversation was over

"So, tell me about your ex girl, what happened with y'all?" I folded my arms, lowkey pouting because I was annoyed from the things he said to me. It was like everything he said was true, I didn't know my worth, but I was slowly learning.

"Dog her out too many times, and she finally left me. At first, I thought she met another nigga, but I realized it was deeper than another nigga. When a woman finally picks herself that's more dangerous than anything. And I think that's what us niggas be more worried about, worried that we going to lose a good girl. I knew I used to think she was my only good girl, but that's like saying it's only one person out here made for you. And that's not true. People placed in your life for reasons, she taught me a lot, how to treat a woman." I have never in my life, heard a nigga admit to his wrongs. Macion would apologize, change for a little, but never acknowledge what he did or correct his wrongs. I was dealing with a grown ass man.

"I should be thanking her," I smirked making him sexily chuckle.

"When you become mine and completely mine, you can thank her." He winked.

For the rest of ride, we just talked about each other lives. He told me about his two little sisters, one was seventeen and the other was twenty-four. He was the oldest at thirty-one. I learned that he was very over protective over his loved ones, and that made me feel good. I loved a nigga that protects his family. When we finally got to his pent house, I was in complete bliss, his home was beautiful. I relaxed in the living room while he cooked dinner, I thought he was playing when he said he could cook, but that food was banging. After we finished eating dinner, he took me to his movie room and now we're cuddled up on the sectional watching *Equalizer 2*.

"Denzel Washington is such a sugar daddy," I chuckled when I felt him pushing me off him. "I mean you could be my sugar daddy too, but we kind of close in age."

"I'll be whatever you want me to be, but is you going to give me sugar?" I looked up at his face and he wore the cutest smirk, showcasing a dimple that I didn't even know as there. I playfully punched him making him laugh. "I was just playing, but to have a sugar daddy you gotta give up the sugar."

"If an old ass daddy touches me, I'm screaming loudly." I spat making him laugh hard as hell. I don't know why he taken me as a joke right now, I was dead ass.

"You stupid as hell for that, yo." He chuckled making me laugh at my own joke. "Going to say I'm screaming loudly. You play too much."

"I am dead ass, I don't want no old ass man."

"You want me?" He asked pulling me onto his lap so that I was straddling him. He didn't even give me a chance to answer him, before his lips crashed against mine. His lips was very soft, they weren't too big or too small, and on top of those great qualities; he knew how to kiss. We continued to kiss before coming up for air, I stared into his eyes with so many thoughts running in through my head, while he stared at me. "You going to get yourself into some shit, you can't get out off."

I stared at him a little longer before climbing off him, he was right I was definitely about to get myself into some shit I couldn't get out of. The crazy part about it was, I don't know if I really want too. *I'm bugging now.*

Ahmeen Santana

I'm Sorry

♡

After the fight I had with True at the hospital, Saaleha would not speak to me. The next day she called me, cursing me the fuck out and snapping on me. She blamed me for him leaving her, as if I forced her to have sex with me. She could've said no. Shit, she shouldn't have come into the bathroom. She knew what she was doing, but that was typical Saaleha, with her naïve ass. She put herself in certain situations and blamed the world for her actions. I saw it as me having sex with my wife. I didn't give a fuck how long I was gone, she was still my wife. And at that moment, she saw it as her having sex with her husband. I knew she did. I was just happy she was allowing me to spend time with my son.

It felt good making up for the missed times, especially since I had been so busy cutting my ties with damn near everyone in the drug business. Don't get me wrong though, I was definitely sticking with arms dealings; it just brought me more money in. It was just, I always told myself I wouldn't be doing this shit forever, so I knew now was the time for me to back out. Kristina had been on some bullshit, calling me every single day, calling herself threatening me, but it was cool. I was going to let her build herself up before I knocked her ass back down to her place. She was just being a hurt bitch.

I had just got to Saleemah's house. It was her birthday, and Saaleha and Reds threw her a cookout. I was surprised when Lee invited me. She tried to say Lil' Meen wanted me there, but I knew she wanted me there too. I still invited someone with me though because I'd be damn if I came alone and True would be there. Saaleha wouldn't be playing me in my face since she was all fake in love with this nigga.

"This is really nice," the chick I brought with me said. I forgot her damn name too, but she was fine. Since I had been back home, I had been waiting on Saaleha, but on my free time, I had been kicking it with this chick. I could never remember her name though; that shit was difficult. I hated difficult ass names. Nodding my head, we walked into Saleemah's home and headed to the backyard. That shit was jumping.

It was like I instantly spotted Saaleha. She was just so beautiful. Over there looking like Pocahontas. Her hair was bone straight, flowing down her back. She wore this hot pink dress that complemented her chocolate skin tone so well. When she faced me, my eyes flew to the small stomach that was finally showing, breaking my heart. My wife was dead ass pregnant by another nigga. Looking back into those gray eyes that I fell in love with, she shook her head before looking at my date. Then her eyes went behind me, and I watched tears form in her eyes.

"Oh no the fuck he didn't!" Reds loud ass prompted me to turn around. It was True with another female. Our eyes connected, and I shook my head, while his jaw tightened. Turning back around, Reds was dragging Lee toward us, while my little sis Minah was right behind them, shaking her head.

"How both of y'all bring bitches? Both of y'all dumb," Minah said as soon as she got close, while looking my date up and down. Listen, Saaleha barely liked my ass right now. I wasn't in the hot seat. True was.

"See naw, that's what *we* not going to do. You not about to bring some bitch up in my best friend, your baby mother's mom house! Have some fucking respect!" Red yelled, making the girl suck her teeth. "Bitch, suck them again and I'll knock all thirty-two down your throat. Play with it."

"Come on, Rambo. Mind your business," Mack said, grabbing her, making me laugh. Reds was definitely Rambo, especially when it came to people she loved.

"Saaleha is my business, and this nigga has her fucked up. Get your bitch out before she gets removed!" Reds ghetto ass yelled before her eyes flew to mine. "Nigga, you too. The fuck is wrong with y'all!"

"What's it to you though? Maybe you need to listen to him and mind—"

"You might not want to do that," Minah interrupted True's chick. I was glad she did, because we all knew Amber's ass wasn't wrapped too tight, like at all.

"I'm just saying, because didn't she fuck her ex," her dumb ass said, making me shake my head. My eyes landed on Saaleha, whose eyes were wide. Then dumb ass Jay was standing there holding onto Khyreema, shaking his head. I didn't even remember him walking over here.

"Bro, you don't pillow talk," Jay said, shaking his head.

"You told her my business?" Saaleha said, walking up on True and homegirl, while Aminah grabbed her arm. "You pillow talked with some bitch about *me*?" She said the last part, pointing at herself.

"Who you calling—" the chick started, but stopped when Saaleha held her hand up and continued to stare at True. I saw all the emotions in Saaleha's face, and I honestly wanted to knock True's clown ass out. I didn't know if it was because I was that protective over Saaleha, but that was what type time I was on.

"Saa, not here, not now. Deal with it later," I said, moving next to her, as I sized True up. Bitch ass nigga.

"Nigga, this between me and her, not you." True stepped in my face. Me and this nigga was the same height, so we were face to face.

"I don't give a fuck who it's between. My nigga, you know me. You know what type of nigga I am. Nobody, and I mean nobody, not even my mom going to disrespect Saaleha. Together or not. That's just how I've been rocking since I met her. And on top of all that, she's *my wife*, the mother of *my son*, and unfortunately, the mother of your unborn child, and your bitch ass in your feelings over some weak shit." I paused before looking at Saaleha. "She belonged to me before she met you, bro. She belonged to me when you first met her too, you just got lucky. And now you got her, and you letting a fuck up make you miss out on a wonderful girl and possibly y'all baby? Nigga, tighten up," I snapped before my eyes traveled to Saaleha's, whose eyes held a look that I couldn't make out. Shaking my head, I looked back at True. "Don't miss out on a family like me, nigga. 'Cause sometimes you can't get that shit back," was all I said before I grabbed Saaleha's hand and headed for the doors.

While we were walking out, I heard Amber's ghetto ass call True a dumb ass nigga, which made me and Saaleha fall out laughing. Her ass was so mean.

"Your date?" Saaleha asked as soon as we got inside of the car.

"Fuck her," I said before backing out the driveway, heading to our favorite place. About thirty minutes later, we had pulled up at the Camden Waterfront, and I went right to the parking spot we always parked at. Saaleha looked around as I put the car in park, then the cutest smile graced her face.

"You remembered."

"Hell yeah. You loved this place. Anytime we needed an escape from reality, we came here. And it seems like that's exactly what you need. An escape," I said, cutting the car off, then looking over at her. She was leaned back with her eyes closed. We sat in silence, basically both in our thoughts, something we both needed.

"He's really hurt," she said finally after five minutes of silence. Sucking my teeth, I shook my head. *Fuck him.* "Ahmeen—"

"I get it, he's hurting, but what about you? You're pregnant, man— you really pregnant." I said the last part more so to myself. I couldn't believe that *my wife* was pregnant by another nigga. Sitting up, Lee ran her hands down the back of my head before speaking.

"I hurt you too—"

"And I hurt you first. I still stand by what I do, but I can say I was on some nut shit for faking my death." I paused, just thinking about the five years I missed. "Pocahontas, I love you, on some real shit. I've never fallen out of love with you. Yes, I fucked up by allowing you to believe I was actually dead. But I want you to know I'm here now. We don't have to be in a relationship, but I'm still your best friend."

"I want you to be around more. I know you have this shit with you, but still come around more, make the effort to be in our lives," she said softly.

"You said our lives." I laughed when she flagged me then rolled her eyes. She could front all she wanted; she knew she missed the kid.

"Boy, don't irk me." She laughed. "But yes, our lives. I would love that. Just no fucking."

"Naw, yo. Your pussy is too good for—"

"No sex, Ahmeen," she demanded. The hell she mean no sex? I mean, yeah, she's pregnant, but damn. No sex?

"How you going to say no to your husband?" I sucked my teeth, looking at her face, which was straight as hell. Like, she wasn't playing no games. "Man, whatever. No sex."

"Thank you." Saaleha leaned over, giving me a hug and a kiss. A passionate kiss. So passionate, my dick got hard. When she pulled away, she licked her lips, causing me to bite my bottom lip.

"Come on with all that after you said no sex." I smirked, and she winked at me. For the rest of the time, we sat in the car just talking for hours until Reds called and said she had Lil' Meen with her. When we finally pulled up to Saaleha's house, it was midnight, and True was sitting on the steps. That look he wore was all familiar too.

"I know that look." I chuckled, putting the car in park.

"What look?" Saaleha said, looking at True.

"The 'I fucked around and hurt Saaleha' look," I said, making her fall out laughing. I wasn't lying. Hurting Saaleha was like hurting yourself because she was so damn sweet. I loved her for that.

"You so dumb for that, yo! But thank you for tonight; it meant a lot to me." She smiled and so did I.

"Stop worrying. Put all your burdens on me. I got you. Even when we not here, I still will have you." I smirked, bringing a smile out of her. Those were the words I said to her when her mom put her out.

"I love you, Meenie." She grabbed my hand.

"Gay ass name. I love you more though, Pocahontas." I smirked. I watched her get out the car and walk past True, whose eyes landed on mine. He gave me a head nod, and I did the same. I didn't know if I could do this friend zone shit, but it was going to have to work. True better stay on his toes because I was going to get my wife back, and that's on *me*.

Thank You, Next.

When we pulled up to my house, my heart dropped seeing True. I didn't want him thinking anything was going on between me and Meen, especially at a time like this. Even though I really needed that talk with Meenie, I honestly hadn't been back to the Camden Waterfront since he *died*. I tried to avoid being places that reminded me of him, reminded me of the past life I lived with him. Being there tonight brought back that little girl who was in love with Ahmeen Santana. The girl who would've done anything for her family. It made me think of the additional family I was creating with True. Then being there tonight brought back so many memories. It reminded me that no matter what, I was forever down for Meen.

It was crazy how someone could hurt you in every way possible, and you'd always stick by their side. I was slowly but surely getting over him faking his death but focusing on the why he moved the way he did. It made being around him easier because at the end of the day, we had a son to continue to raise together.

"Lee." True's voice interrupted my thoughts when we walked inside the house. I wasn't really trying to hear anything he had to say. Bitch ass had the nerve to bring another bitch to *my* mom's house. Turning around, I looked him up and down before scoffing and continued to my room. He was right behind me too, looking like a sad puppy. He had life fucked up if he thought what he pulled earlier was cool.

Walking into my room, I slipped out of my Tory Burch sandals before pulling my dress over my head. I wanted to shower, but my ass was too sleepy to do anything. So, going into my top drawer, I pulled out one of True's t-shirts and pulled it over my head and laid down, all while his eyes stayed on me. He could kiss my nice, round ass. I didn't have shit to say to him. I grabbed the remote, turning the television on and getting comfortable. I tried to sneak a look at True, who was standing there looking good as fuck and was just staring at me. I watched him walk over to me, feeling my breath get caught in my throat because that was how nervous he made me. He pulled the covers back, then stared down my body, licking his lips.

"You just going to act like a nigga not here? Then wear my shit to sleep?" he asked softly before his hands flew to the hem of the shirt and pulled it up.

"True!" I yelped when his cold hands touched my skin. He placed his hands on my stomach and rubbed. He got down on his knees then placed soft kisses on my stomach. The other day we found out we were having a girl, and goodness was I happy. Finally, a girl in my fiasco I called life.

"Why your mom tripping out on me? She the one who—"

"Get the fuck off me!" I pushed him away, making him chuckle. "That shit not funny. Get off me."

"I was just playing, calm down." He stood before he started to strip out his clothes, down to his briefs. My eyes flew to my favorite part of his body except his lips, and he smiled. "Scoot over some."

"Not until you apologize," was all I said before I folded my arms and pouted. He had life messed up if he thought he didn't have to apologize. I didn't care what I did; he was dead wrong for bringing some bird to my mother's house.

"You got that one. I was on some nut shit for bringing her to your mom's house, Lee."

"You damn right you were, and you wrong for pillow talking with that bitch." I sucked my teeth, making him chuckle before nudging me so that I could move over.

"That was my cousin though, no cap. She wanted to meet you," He shrugged chuckling, making my head snap in his direction. He fell out laughing as if something was funny.

"You petty," I mumbled before shaking my head.

"I meant to ask you the other day, does that number still text you?" he asked in regard to that unknown number. I shook my head 'no' because they really hadn't since that day, and he nodded. "Good. I tracked it and it was from a burner phone from out Mexico."

Shrugging my shoulders because I didn't know anybody from Mexico, I turned to face the TV, when I felt his lips on the side of my face. "What you want, man?"

"I want you," he mumbled before he climbed on top of me. Balancing himself on his forearms, he hovered over me, being careful so he wouldn't lean on my stomach, and stared into my eyes. I felt my body getting hot and ready like Little Caesars Pizza; the effects this man had over me. "Can I have you?" he whispered against my lips. He wouldn't kiss me until I answered him. I nodded my head because at this point, I needed him to give me that vitamin D!

"Yes. You can ha—" was all I could get out before his lips crashed against mine. We kissed like two dogs in heat before I felt my panties being slipped off and the head of his member struggling against my entrance. No matter how many times we had sex, I wasn't used to his size. Then on top of me being pregnant, sometimes it hurt more than it usually did. I was so ready for this ride because I needed this. My ass had been horny as hell. I was showing out tonight, and that's a fact!

"What are we doing?" I asked True once we finished having sex. We had been laying there for about fifteen minutes, just relaxing. But I needed to know; he was so back and forth with me now. I get it, I messed up by cheating on him with Meen, but I didn't deserve to have my feelings played with.

"What you mean? We're chilling." He shifted his body so that his arm was draped over my stomach, and he started rubbing it. His hands stayed on my stomach. It was so cute because it reminded me of Ahmeen. *See, no, Saaleha. You have to stop thinking of your fake dead husband and focus on your baby dad,* I thought to myself before responding.

"Okay, but what are we doing all together? Like one day you're here, one day you're not, so…" My voice trailed off. I turned around to face him, needing to look in his eyes. I needed to make sure he wasn't going to lie to me.

Taking a deep sigh, he sat up before running his hands through his now messy bun, then he tugged on his beard before speaking. "I'm just not over it, Lee. Every time I think I am, I'm really not. I love you and shit, but I don't know if I can forgive you. Well, just not yet. Who knows how I'll feel once the baby gets here."

"Okay. Well, we'll figure this out when the baby gets here. You can leave." I mumbled before getting out of bed and heading to the bathroom with him hot on my heels.

"Lee, it's—"

"I cheated on you, I get it. I said I was sorry, and that's not enough. I get it. I'm trying so damn hard here, but it's not my fault that Meen faked his death. I didn't kn—"

"How didn't you know? He's your husband!" he interrupted me. His face was rock hard while I was pretty sure mine was completely confused. "You could've been faking this shit, just how he was."

"Faking this shit?" I angrily chuckled. Looking to the ceiling, I counted to ten just to calm myself down. Had to remember that I was pregnant. "Get out."

"What?"

"Get the hell out my house. I was faking? Faking what exactly? I spent five fucking years on my lonesome, taking care of my son, trying to figure out what the hell happened to Ahmeen! That pain was real; that pain was inevitable. I wouldn't have wished what I went through on nobody! And now you are sitting up here basically calling me a liar because my stupid ass baby dad lied?" I screamed, standing on my tippy toes with my finger in his face. "You got me fucked up. Get out."

"Lee, I didn't mean it like that. I was just angry. Listen, we can work this out after the baby. I don't want to stress you and shit."

He pulled me into him, but I pushed him off. He just tried me, like really bad. "Come on, Lee,"

"Just go home," was all I said before starting the shower. I felt him still standing there watching me, before I heard him suck his teeth.

"I love you," he spoke before leaving me there. As much as I wanted to cry, I was tired of being a weak bitch. I was tired of people treating me like I was naïve and like I was just anybody. I was not perfect, I fucked up, but I was a damn good person, and I didn't deserve none of the shit Ahmeen or True offered me. They were lucky I was pregnant and didn't have time for none of these niggas and their bullshit. I was on some new, improved shit with myself. I was a mother and about to have another baby. I couldn't be distracted by these niggas. Thank you, next!

True Taylor

Mad Stalkers.

I hadn't talked to or saw Saaleha in about two weeks, and I had been losing my damn mind. When I said she was not fucking with me, I meant just that. She hadn't answered my calls, unlinked her calendar from my phone so I wouldn't when her appointments were, and hadn't been home for me to pop up. Only time she texted me was when it was updates about the baby. Other than that, she didn't respond or acknowledge any of my messages. Her mom, Saleemah, wasn't even fucking with me. Only person who kept me updated about Saaleha was Amber and Lil' Meen. Lil' Meen told me they'd been spending time with Ahmeen, and that shit bothered me more than anything because he was the reason why we were in this predicament now. I didn't even know how she was upset with me. I was the one who should be doing the ignoring. She cheated on me.

"I'm glad you decided to meet me, papi," Kristina said as she sat in front of me. I had met her in Miami because this bitch was sending threats toward Saaleha. Sucking my teeth, I watched her take a seat. I wasn't even going to lie, she looked good as hell. The way this soft pink, tight-fitted dress complemented her vanilla skin tone, it clung to her curves perfectly.

"I don't think I had much of a choice, now did I?" I asked, fixing my tie because I was so ready to jump over this table. I hated bitches that just couldn't accept a breakup. She had to do the most. She sat there with the biggest grin on her face as if she'd won something.

"No, not really. I'm glad you're smart though. I didn't want to have to come after *mi amor*." She brushed her pink tongue across her bottom lip, before pulling it between her teeth.

Different Sides Of The Game 2

"What do you want?"

"I want you to cancel that *puta* Saaleha and get back with me." She smiled, her weird ass. "I know her husband isn't really dead, he's alive, which should make you want to just come back home to me." Her delusional ass smirked. "Or, I could just tell my people to end her and then you'll have no—"

She didn't even get the rest of her sentence out before I had her choked up, feet dangling, and my gun pointed under her chin. Her men had their guns drawn on me, but I didn't give a damn about all that. She had me fucked up, threatening Saaleha's life. If I knew she was bluffing, I wouldn't have reacted this way. But Kristina was a true killer, and I knew what she and her family was capable of.

"Now, what the fuck was you saying?" I barked in her ear, while she tried to gasp for air. "What was all that tough shit you were talking? You going to do what?"

"They'll kill you if I say so. Let me go now, True!" she barked out. Chuckling lightly, I pushed my gun more into her chin, grabbing her neck tighter.

"As long as I take you out, I'm cool. We'll both die today." I smirked when her eyes widened. She was going to learn not to fuck with me today.

"Tr-True, please, let me go," she mumbled before her eyes flew to her men. "Lower your weapons, *ahora!*" They put their weapons down, and I dropped her to the ground. She lay there, holding her neck gasping for air. Getting down to her level, I gripped her hair around my hand, jerking her neck back.

"Listen here, I bet not hear from you ever again. I don't even want you to think about me. Know that I will kill you with my bare hands if something happens to Saaleha or her family. I can promise you that," I whispered in her ear before pulling away and looking into her eyes. I saw the fear flash across her face. I needed her to know I wasn't playing with her crazy ass.

"Okay, I got it," was all she said before I got up, leaving her on the ground holding her neck. I didn't take threats well, especially not ones directed toward the mother of my unborn. I'd go out

Page | 113

blazing over Saaleha's ass, no cap. I didn't trust Kristina. I knew no matter what I said to her, she was going to try me. So, I already knew I was going to add her to the list of who I had to keep my eye on. I was ready to just end both Kristina and Kiera's lives. I hated bitter bitches.

"You're the last person I expected to be here," Meen said when he opened the door for me. "If you're looking for my wife, she's not here." He smirked, trying to be the fuck smart, per usual.

"I already knocked your ass out before. Quit playing with me. I'm here on some business shit," I spat before pushing past him into the house. You would think this nigga had been living here for a minute. The crib was nicely, fully furnished out Flourtown, PA. I would say he kept his head way above water for those five years he played dead.

"Stop acting like a little bitch," he spoke as we both took a seat inside the living room. He was always trying me. "But what's good?"

"You know some bitch name Kristina?" I asked.

"Yeah, my old bitch. Well, our old bitch. We just enjoy the same chicks, huh?" Meen spat. So that's how Kristina knew he was still alive. Her hoe ass. "But what's good with her? I haven't seen her since I left DR."

"She's threatening to kill Lee, if I don't stop messing with her," I said, watching his face twist up. I knew this nigga was about to say some shit to piss me off.

"Then stop messing with her," he said, making a face as if I was tripping or something. I wanted to rock his shit so bad, but I didn't have time to be fighting him and shit. We had to handle Kristina, and I said we because she threatened Saaleha, and I knew he was pissed about the shit just as I was.

"That's my baby mom, nigga. How th— you know what, we really need to handle this bitch. I'm pretty sure she threatened you too, and you know you can't put nothing past a crazy bitch."

"You know what, you right. I know that bitch, and I know what's she capable of. We do gotta handle her." We sat there coming up with a solid plan so that we could handle Kris. We knew we would have to come up with something concrete because, after earlier, I knew her father would be calling me soon. Sitting here rapping with him felt like when he was a kid and used to come to me for advice. This time, he was wiser, smarter, and not as hot-headed as he used to be. It was just now we shared the same love for the same girl.

"So, what you planning on doing with Saa? I mean, you know I'm back, and I'm not about to let her go all easily." Meen shrugged while leaning back onto the sofa. I needed to get out of here before I knocked his ass out again. He talked to me about Saaleha as if everything was cool and sweet. *Nigga, we are beefing over the same girl; that's the mother of both of our children,* I thought to myself as I stared at his dumb ass.

"You never going to get her back where you had her, bitch boy." I threw my middle finger up before walking out his house. Jumping in my car, I headed to Saaleha's house. I didn't have time for her bullshit any longer. I missed her. When I pulled up to her home, which was about twenty minutes away from Meen's, I hopped out and walked up to her door. I wasn't knocking this time either. Using the pin code, I walked into her house like I paid bills in here.

"Oooh, Lee, you in trouble!" Minah and Reds yelled out when they saw me walking into the house. Saaleha turned around with wide eyes before looking down at my hand. I was carrying her bumpers that she left in my car. She'd been asking for them for like a week.

"Oh, now you come with my shit. Got me out here looking a mess!" Lee jumped up, wobbling toward me. I chuckled just watching her little ass all pissed off and cute. When she finally got toward me, I pulled her into me, surprising her.

"Get rid of your company and meet me upstairs," was all I said before kissing her lips and walking away with a smirk on my face.

"You heard your man. Come on, Minah. She about to get that pussy waxed, okurrt!" I heard Reds stupid self say, making me chuckle. About fifteen minutes later, I heard Saaleha mumbling some smart shit before she entered the room. Her lip went up as if she was disgusted by me, before she rolled her eyes hard as hell and walked toward the bed. I watched her climb into the bed, pressing her back against the headboard, then folded her arms over her stomach. Her cute ass.

"So you call yourself being mad at me?" I asked her, while pulling my shirt over my head. I undid my jeans before allowing them to sag a little. Her eyes stayed on mine until I made it over to the bed, and I placed kisses over her stomach. I missed feeling my daughter kick. "You don't hear me?"

"Nobody mad at you, True. I just don't fuck with you," she said matter-of-factly.

"Well, I miss you, and I want us to get back together." I smiled when her eyes widened before she chuckled lightly. "What's funny?"

"You're funny. Now all of sudden you want to get back together? Have you forgiven me?" She stared at me with her head cocked to the side. Why she had to worry about the extra shit? Shouldn't she be jumping for joy? I knew she missed me just as much as I missed her.

"I mean, not fully, but I can, and I will. So, what do you say? Just come home, Lee." I kissed her lips lightly, hoping that this was enough. I really wanted this to work between us, I needed it too. Because I knew after she has this baby I'm going fall deeper in love with her.

"You want to get back together because you don't want Ahmeen to have full access to me." She read me. She was so difficult nowadays. "So, no. We are not getting back together right now. We will co-parent, and when you finally truly forgive me and won't be holding it over my head, I'll consider it. I want a happy pregnancy. I don't want to constantly argue. Ahmeen is here, he's my sons' father, so he will be around more than you know it. There's nothing I can do about any of this, but I need you to get over this because I am truly sorry for hurting you. I promise you. But I'm not getting back into a relationship with you until you fully forgive me."

"Why you so perfect?" I sat on the bed, pulling her closer to me. She chuckled before placing a soft kiss onto my lips.

"Far from perfect, but really smart," she said between our kisses. She was right about this. I had to work on forgiving her if I wanted this to work, and I really did.

Kiera Mitchell

Envy Me.

♡

I was back in Philly now, lying in my bed, relaxing. Omar hadn't spoke to me since I told him that I would be working with Kristina, but it was okay. I had something for that ass. Kristina told me that Mack killed Cherrelle. I didn't know how she knew that, but she did. So, when I told him this shit, I knew he was going to be on board. We could get Amber's ass too. Kill two birds with one stone. I'd give Omar a couple days to cool off before I tell him. I'd put the pussy on him before anything, and he'd do whatever I said. I'd called Saaleha too, the other day, and that bitch ignored my calls. I didn't know what got into her, but fuck her bitches. I had got my mind right on that vacation and been kicking it with Kristina. She was like my new best friend and shit; well, with benefits. She turned me out, okurrt! I knew why True wouldn't leave her alone before he met Lee.

I had gone by the shop the other day to pick up the rest of my things, and boy, was I happy as hell Amber and Saaleha weren't there. I didn't have time for neither one of their asses; plus, I knew Amber wanted to fight me because she'd texted me all the time saying when she sees me it's on sight. It was so funny to me, because I taught those bitches how to fight, and now they wanted to rumble me. Yeah, okay. They were so bitter and jealous. It was cute. Anyway, I was getting out the shower when my phone went off. Picking it up, I sucked my teeth. My mom had been calling me for two weeks now after I stopped dropping money into her account. All these years later, she never got off drugs with her dumb ass. Picking up the phone, I took a deep breath. I didn't feel like her ass, for real.

"Hello?" I answered, rolling my eyes as if she could see me.

"I've been calling your narrow behind for weeks now. What the fuck is wrong with you?" Keisha yelled into the phone. I paid all her bills and kept money in her pockets, and this was how her bum ass talked to me. One would think I didn't do anything for her.

"Is there something you need, Keisha?" I sighed. I didn't feel like talking to Keisha's ass or listening to her smart remarks. She had the right one today.

"You damn right. I need some money!"

"I just transferred ten thousand into your account. What happened to that?" I sucked my teeth. I swore she blew money fast. Like, how much did drugs really cost, because it was no way. I wasn't even blowing ten thousand a day when I was on pills. Shit, I barely blew a thousand. She was bugging.

"Hoe, that was two weeks ago. Send me some money, damn! It's the least you can fucking do!"

"The least I can do? You serious?" I asked, shocked as hell. She had some nerve. All that I did for her, and she said it was the least I could do? I couldn't believe her junkie ass.

"Yes I am. The fuck!" Keisha yelled.

"Everything I've ever done in my life was because of you. I'm the way I am because of you!" I yelled back. I tried to stop the tears from falling, but they wouldn't. It was crazy that my mom used to be so sweet and lovely, and now she acted as if I wasn't, even her daughter. My mom and I used to be so close until she started her drug habit; it tore the whole family apart.

"Stop the fucking lies. The shit you go through is because of you, with your shady ass. If I told your ass to jump off a cliff, you gonna do it? Send me my damn money, Kiera, or I'll call Saaleha and—"

"Fuck you." I barked before hanging up on her. I didn't have time for her bullshit. My mom was the first person to break my heart. And I would never forgive her for that shit, no matter how hard I tried. She broke me.

After calming myself down, I moisturized my skin before putting some clothes on. By the time I was done, somebody was knocking on my door. Sucking my teeth, I let out a deep sigh. I did not feel like Omar today. Stomping down the stairs, I rolled my eyes before swinging the door open. Nobody was there. I didn't have time for these little kids in my neighborhood. About to walk away, I looked down and it was a box with my name on it. Looking around, I smiled, picking it up. Omar must be coming to his senses. Walking into my dining room, I placed the box on the table before opening it.

"Oh, my g— Ronnie?" I jumped back, covering my mouth. Someone sent me Ronnie's freaking head! "What the fuck, what the fuck, what the—" I paused when I saw a note. I walked over to the note with tears clouding my eyes.

Everything done in the dark, comes to the light.

Throwing the paper down, I ran upstairs to call Omar.

"Stop calling me, Kiera!"

"Omar, please. Somebody dropped Ronnie's head off at my door. Please, Omar. I'm scared!" I cried hard. I had never been so scared in my life. "Omar!"

"I don't know what you expect me to do. Better call that bitch Kristina. I told you everything you do was going to catch up to you!" he yelled before hanging up on me. He was such a bitch. Scrolling to Rico's name, I called him. The first two calls went straight to voicemail, before he answered the third call.

"Why you keep calling me, Kiera? You're pissing my girl off," he said calmly.

"Rico, somebody... somebody dropped that nigga Ronnie's head off at my door. Please come over." I cried in the phone.

"What you mean?" he asked.

"Somebody dropped off a package, and when I opened it, it was Ronnie's head with a note saying I'm next. Rico, please. I'm so scared, and I don't deserve to die." I was so fucking scared, I swear.

Different Sides Of The Game 2

"Ard, I'm on my way," he spoke into the phone before he hung up. I was happy as hell he was about to come here. I didn't know what to do. Whoever dropped Ronnie's head off was a fucked-up person. I didn't deserve none of this. I couldn't believe Omar hung up on me, because if this was in regard to Ahmeen's death, he was going down too! But whoever wrote that note was right; everything that was done in the dark definitely comes to the light. I didn't have time to be waiting for Rico, I had to get out of town now and fast. So, I sent Kristina a text telling her what happen and ran upstairs to pack my things. I wasn't about to die, at all. Throwing my clothes in my bag, my phone went off indicating I had a text. Reading the text from Kris, it read.

Plane takes off in one hour, better be there.

Aminah Santana

It's either HER or ME?

"Ard, I'm on my way," Rico said into the phone before he hung up, shocking the hell out of me. I sat there with my legs bouncing up and down, as I stared at the man I started to love about to go to his *ex's* rescue. "Don't look at me like that. I would do the same shit for you, Minah."

"Don't look at you like that? You have me so fucked up. You think you about to walk out this door and go to that bitch's house because she asked you to!" I yelled, jumping up, getting all in his face; well, my head was in the middle of his chest. "Is that what you think you about to do?"

"Aminah, go 'head. You blowing my shit. The damn girl said somebody dropped a dead nigga's head off at her door!" he yelled, making me flinch. I stared at him in disbelief before backing up and nodding.

"Well, I'm leaving, and don't fucking call me. Stupid ass running to the grimiest bitch defense!" I yelled out. "That bitch set my brother up! That's why his head was dropped off!" I screamed as I gathered myself. I didn't even mean to tell him all that, but it slipped. I didn't care. I lived without my brother for all these years behind that snake bitch. After I finally decided to talk to Ahmeen, he told me about everything, and I couldn't believe her. I knew I didn't like her for a reason.

"What you mean, Aminah? Come here, yo!" he barked, grabbing me by my arm. He searched my eyes, trying to see if I was playing, but as the tears fell out my eyes, he knew I was serious.

"I suffered for years, thinking my brother died. Come to find out, that bitch is the one who did that shit. She drove that car! Now you wanna run to her rescue? Fuck you!" I screamed. I knew he didn't know, but it was the thought of my man running to another chick's rescue.

"Aminah, just calm—"

"But nah, it's way deeper than that. The nigga that I'm in love with was about to jump to another bitch because she said so. That's the problem. So when I become number one to you, hit me up," I said, grabbing my things, while his stupid ass stood there as if he was in disbelief. He grabbed my arm, and I snatched away. I walked out the room with him hot on my heels. He stood there with his arms folded, looking all good. Rolling my eyes, I put my shoes on, grabbing my bag. He snatched my arm again.

"You are number one to me. Man, chill the fuck out. Fuck Kiera. I just know how scary that shit can be, yo." He pleaded with me, but I didn't want to hear that shit. "I'm not letting you leave, on my life I'm not. You can take your ass back upstairs, pick a room, but you not leaving this house," he snapped, staring at me, making my panties get wet. I stared at him for a little because I was lowkey loving the way he bossed up on me.

"So what, if you know how that shit be? She's not your concern. I am. So if you don't have this shit figured out by now, then maybe we're wasting our time."

"What, Minah? You bugging. I don't give a fuck about her. She cheated on me! I just know what comes in this world. Shit like that fucks with your mental. I'm with you, and you know it. So kill all this leaving shit, 'cause you not going nowhere. Sit your ass down somewhere!" he snapped. His face was red, and his veins were popping out his arm and neck. He was pissed. I had never seen him this mad. Sucking my teeth, I pouted before looking around.

"Fine. I'm sleeping in the guestroom downstairs." I pulled away from him, rolling my eyes. When I walked away, he smacked my butt before gripping it. "No, get off me." I pushed him off me, only for him to pull me back into him then kiss my neck.

Different Sides Of The Game 2

"You mad at me?" He kissed my forehead. "Huh? Don't be mad at me, baby. It's always going to be you. Nobody else, trust me on that shit." He picked me up, wrapping my legs around him. He leaned me against the wall.

"I'm not even playing games with you. As soon as I feel like you're moving funny, it's a wrap. I'm out." I smiled, wrapping my arms around his neck and kissing him passionately.

"I'm not out to hurt you, La Bella," he whispered before he unwrapped my legs from around his waist. My arms were still wrapped around his neck, so I was swinging a little. He pulled my sweat pants down before releasing my new bestie. Yes, I lost my virginity finally, and baby, I couldn't stay off my man. At all. I knew what I was missing for twenty-four years, then on top of that, my sex partner was just amazing.

"Shit," I moaned as he entered me, and I dropped my arms from around his neck and leaned my head against the wall. He stroked inside of me deeper and deeper, while spreading my cheeks apart so that he could apply pressure on my g-spot.

"Dig your nails in my back," he groaned before kissing me. That was another thing. I didn't know why he loved pain when we were having sex. I mean, I liked it when he choked me, but he always wanted my nails in his back. I think papis just liked pain, freak asses.

"Baby, I'm cumming," I moaned as I felt myself erupt on his dick. My body shook hard before I felt weak.

"Damn, Minah. I'm about to cum too. Give me another one," he said as he placed his hand on the wall above my head, and stroked inside of me, matching my grinds. Pushing him up, I unwrapped my legs, and he placed me on the floor. Getting on my knees, I started to suck his member just how he taught me.

"Cum in my mouth." I stuck my tongue out, looking up at him in his eyes. His mouth opened before he gripped my hair and came hard in my mouth, and I swallowed everything up. Snatching me up from the floor, he kissed me passionately, making me chuckle.

Page | 124

"You trying to make me marry you, girl?" he asked with his forehead leaned against mine. Nodding my head, 'yes', he chuckled before kissing me on my lips. "Come on. Go pack a bag."

"Wh-what you mean? Where we going?" I stuttered, watching him head for the stairs.

"Put your money where your mouth is, La Bella. Come on; we going to Vegas. We'll see if you still want to be my wife then." He winked, leaving me stuck. What did he mean put my money where my mouth is? If this nigga proposes to me on this damn trip, y'all, I'm going to say yes, then have a heart attack! I guess we just going to have to see. Vegas, here I come.

"You sure you want to do this, CoCo? This is marriage, not a relationship." I stared at him, as we sat in the rental outside of a very nice chapel. I can't believe I allowed him to talk me into getting married, but fuck it I was ready. I was ready to become Mrs. Aminah Vega, that's how good to me he was. It might be too soon, but that didn't phase the either one of us.

"Don't tell me you're bitching," he leaned his head against the headrest making me chuckle at the face he was giving me. Rolling my eyes, I stuck my middle finger up before climbing out the car. We walked inside of the chapel, and he set everything up, I was so nervous. I can't believe we're about to get married, I wanted my mom here, my family here. But we can do that later, I was about to get married and couldn't be happier.

"La Bella, I love you, I know this isn't your ideal marriage, but I promise to make it up to you. I don't have no extra long shit to say, but know I appreciate and love you more than you think. You've been everything I needed since I met you, I love you the most for that." He said making me shake my head.

"CoCo, I want to thank you for coming in my life and being my superman. Thank you for protecting and loving me flaws and all. I won't be all long because you know I could pour my heart to you. I'm just ready to spend forever with you and have some pretty mixed babies." I stuck my tongue out making him chuckled.

Different Sides Of The Game 2

"Can you hurry this process up, I'm trying to get her fine ass to the honeymoon."

"I now pronounce you, Mr. and Mrs. Vega, you may kiss your—" The pastor didn't even get to finish before Rico was pulling me into him and placing a soft kiss on my lips. He carried me bridal style to the car, I really was a married woman now. I never even thought about getting married at twenty-four, but here I was.

"Where we going now, husband?" I smiled brightly just thinking how I was about to 'my husband' everybody to death.

"Paris, you ready?" Hell yeah I was ready, I was ready to take on the world as long as I had Rico by my side, I was good. Nodding my head, I sat back and thought about my new life with my husband, I wasn't worried about my mom or family. For once I was doing something that didn't involve the approval of my family, I was doing it because I wanted too. And it felt great.

Jayceon "Jay" Johnson
Where I Wanna Be

I was laying inside of Khyreema's bed. She had her head on my chest with her leg across mine. Her mouth was slightly ajar as she softly snored. I stared down at her, taking in her beauty. It was crazy how much I really loved this girl. She was so laid back and chilled, workaholic, and too close to perfect. She was the total opposite of Rhonda's ratchet ass. Speaking of Rhonda, she'd been blowing my phone up since the day I left her crib. Trust me, I had her ass on the blocklist, but that didn't stop her from calling me from everybody and their moms' phone. That's why today, I was going to go by there and end things correctly, but I knew Khy wasn't going to let me go alone.

"Stop staring at me, babe," she said, making me chuckle. She stirred a little bit before she faced me with her eyes still closed but with her lips poked out for a kiss. Leaning forward, I kissed her soft, plump lips, and she smiled before opening those big, beautiful eyes. "Why are you up so early?"

"Khy, baby, it's eleven in the morning." I chuckled, making her pick up her phone and jump up. "She ate breakfast, and I took her to school. Saaleha picking her up," I said, reading her mind. Shaking her head, she chuckled lightly before laying back down.

"You are so perfect. Thank you. I can't believe I slept through my alarm." She yawned before laying back on my chest. I ran my hand through her hair that was now wavy from our sex session last night. "I'm hungry."

"We can go get some breakfast from Sabrina's. I got some errands to run today though. You wanna come with me?" I didn't even know why I asked her that, knowing her little clingy ass was going to say yes.

"You know I do. Is that even a question?" Her cute face was balled up, forcing a small chuckle out of me. "What do you have to do?" she asked, getting out of bed and walking toward me. I was afraid to bring up Rhonda, but I knew I had to. I didn't have time for Khyreema's extra ass.

"Take you out to breakfast, run by the tattoo shop to make sure everything go— what?" I stopped when the cutest grin graced Khy Baby face.

"'Cause, babe, you're finally about to allow the world to see your talent. I can't wait so you can give me my first tattoo." She smiled brightly. I wasn't going to front either, I was happy as hell too. Meen and I were on our shit about this tattoo shop. It was our plan to do before he 'died'. We had found a building back then and everything, then that nut shit took place and set us back. So it felt good to be back at it. If I wasn't good at anything, tattoos were something I was great at.

"What you going to get? Me and Kay's name?" I inquired. She rolled her eyes before sticking her middle finger up, and walked away.

"Boy, please. You get my name, I'll get yours!" she spat before walking into the bathroom. "Anyway, what else?"

"Stop by Rhonda's," was all I said before her head snapped in my direction.

"Run that shit back."

"She keeps calling me and shit, so we going to go by and set shit straight. You going to be there, so I don't know why you about to trip." I kissed her cheek before starting the shower. I knew she wanted to say more, but she didn't, and I was cool with that.

The last thing I needed or wanted to do was argue with my girl over some bullshit. After we showered, we went to Sabrina's Café to get some breakfast, then headed over to the tattoo shop. When we walked in, and Khyreema spun around like a big kid before the cutest grin blessed her face. She walked over to me before placing her head in my chest. A few seconds later, I heard her sniffle. Pulling away from her, I gripped her shoulders to look at her face; this nigga was crying.

"Babe, what the hell you crying for?" I balled my face up, and she sucked her teeth and wiped her eyes.

"Because baby, I'm so proud of you! Look at this." She pouted, poking her bottom lip out. "Jay, baby, I am soooo proud of you!" She pulled me into her, making me chuckle. We were hugging before Meen walked in with a very pregnant Saaleha. She could deny him all she wanted, but we all knew she wanted her man back.

"Get yo' cuffing ass outta here." Meen chuckled, giving me a handshake. Lee popped him on his arm, making me chuckle. "Don't start, yo!"

"Y'all like Ike and Tina nowadays, and we all know Lee is Ike of the two," I cracked, making Khy baby laugh. Lee stuck her tongue out before giving me a high five.

"You knew, period," Lee joked while Meen stood there, pouting. "Ah, sike, naw. Stop playing with my baby daddy, Jay."

"Husband."

"Nope, baby daddy," Saaleha corrected Meen, sticking her tongue out. Chuckling, I shook my head because they'd been going at it since he came back. Safe to say, sis didn't mess with him like that.

While the girls gave themselves a tour of the shop, Meen and I discussed business in regard to the shop. It was the first time in the longest that we didn't talk about shit involving the streets but things that involved keeping our pockets laced, legally. After we finished going over the hiring dates and our grand opening date, Khyreema and I left, heading to Rhonda's house. When we pulled up, I took a deep breath. I didn't feel like the drama that was about to come my way right now, but I needed to set some things straight.

"Amen," I heard Khy say, making my head snap in her direction. Scrunching up her face, she looked me up and down before saying, "What?"

"Were you just praying?" I asked, and she nodded her head before taking her seat belt off. "For what?"

"To give me the strength and will power to stop from going up side this hoe head if she gets besides herself. I don't have time to be going to jail. Kay needs me, and I don't like orange, tan, or dark blue," her crazy ass said, making me chuckle.

"You know I'll always bail you out." I kissed her cheek, making her chuckle.

"Yeah, I know, but we can save that money for this Birkin you're about to buy me when we leave here," she stated before getting out the car, making me chuckle, following behind her. I got out the car before she rounded the car. Walking hand in hand with Khyreema, when we got to the door, I pulled out my key, and she slapped my hand.

"What you hitting me for, Khy baby?" I sucked my teeth, making her roll my eyes.

"Because that's why her ass so comfortable. You're walking up in her crib like you own this shit. No. What you going to do is knock on the door like the guest you are, and wait for her to open the door," she spat. I stared at her for a little because I was liking how she was bossing up on me. "Why are you just staring at me and not knocking?"

Chuckling, I did as I was told and knocked on the door. We waited for about two minutes before Rhonda came to the door, looking like a fucking snack, man. She was in these booty shorts and a tank top that showed a little of her stomach. I must've been staring too hard because Khyreema smacked me in the back of my head, making Rhonda smirk.

"The fuck?"

"I saw you staring. Don't do that, Jayceon." Khyreema rolled her eyes before looking at Rhonda, who was still smirking. Noticing that I just disrespected my girl, I pulled her in to my side and kissed her face.

"You right. I'm sorry." Now it was her turn to smirk because Rhonda's face balled right up. Sucking her teeth, she folded her arms while looking Khyreema up and down.

"What do you want? And why didn't you use your key?" Rhonda said, trying to be smart.

"Because he doesn't live here, shawty. Matter of fact give her that key back," Khy demanded, making me chuckle. She was getting carried away with this bossing up shit. But I was going to do what she said and handle all that other shit later with her hype self.

"So, you bring a bitch to my house and then you let her tell you what to do?" Rhonda chuckled before making eye contact with Khyreema. "See baby, what me and Jay have beats everything y'all built within the year y'all been fucking. This nigga loves me. I've been down for him since we were seventeen. He will never throw me away for some new bitch, trust me. I'm letting him have his fun before he returns home. You'll never be me."

Laughing hard as hell, as if Rhonda said the funniest thing ever, Khy baby looked up at me and pointed at Rhonda. "You hear her, baby? She said that she's allowing you to have fun before you return home. Ha." She laughed before her face got serious. "See, that's the problem with y'all women nowadays. Y'all be letting these niggas do y'all in and allowing them back home because now that dog done roaming. But listen here, you're absolutely right. I'll never be a weak bitch like you. Do you know how dumb you just sounded?

Girl, he doesn't love you. He came here today because he felt like it's the least he could do since you won't stop calling. Secondly, he threw you away when he came to his senses and came to me. So do yourself a favor and just stop calling my man, sis. It's over between you and him." Let me tell you something, my dick was bricked up listening to my little baby.

"You gon' let her talk to me like that, Jay?" Rhonda spat with tears filling her eyes. Shrugging my shoulders because there wasn't nothing left to be said, she chuckled, wiping the tears that didn't fall and nodded her head. "It' cool. Go 'head, be with this black ass bitch. Like I said, baby, he'll be back. He always comes back!" she snapped before slamming her door in our faces. I looked over at Khyreema who wore a weird expression before she looked up at me.

"You good?" I asked, grabbing her hand as we walked down the stairs.

"Yeah. I just know she's about to come with all this drama. I can feel it." She wasn't lying either. I knew Rhonda, and I knew this wasn't going to be the last of her. She went hard for me. I just hoped that Khyreema wouldn't fold under pressure when the time came.

Amber "Reds" Wright

Are you down to be a distraction, baby?

Lately, Montez and I had been spending so much time together. I was truly feeling him. I didn't know how we'd been doing it, but I'd been fitting him in my crazy schedule, and he'd been fitting me into his. Macion hadn't been asking any questions, and I doubt he had any suspicions, because I'd been using Aminah as my excuse every time. And it made it better because Aminah finally got her own place, so now my lies be coming through. I couldn't use Saaleha because she lived across the damn street, plus she'd been spending her time with her son, her husband, and her baby daddy. My sis's life was complicated as hell right now. So, I'd been taking my infidelities over to Aminah's house; since she moved in with Rico. It worked out perfectly for me, especially since Mack and Rico barely knew each other. I also think Minah be pillow talking and told him about me stepping out with Montez. Her little snitch ass.

Anyway, I was on my way over to Minah's house to spend time with Montez. We'd been on a lot of dates, but we'd never had sex or anything like that. *So it's not really cheating, right?* I asked myself. We'd just been spending time. I'm not emotionally attached, I don't think. I had just got to Minah's house. Pulling down my visor, I applied some lip gloss and fixed my hair. In the middle of me fixing myself up, Saaleha started calling.

"Yes, Lee?"

"You out being a hoe?" Her voice came through the speakers in my car, making me laugh.

"I am not a hoe."

"Oh yeah, you a cheating hoe. My bad." She chuckled. Disconnecting my phone from my car, I got out the car.

"I didn't even have sex with him," I mumbled while getting out the car and grabbing my overnight bag. I was nervous as hell, honestly.

"So you telling me you aren't thinking about it? I mean, that nigga is fine, so I know you want to," she said matter-of-factly. I couldn't stand her dumb ass.

"Why you judging?"

"Ain't nobody judging your ass, but I know you about to stay the night with him. So I know you going to fuck him, so be real with me and yourself."

"How about you be real with me and yourself and go back to your husband, because we all know you want to," I spat.

"Okay, lil' Kiera, I'm just saying. Don't go fucking up your home because you want a quick nut. Stop saying you forgive Mack when you're doing all this because you haven't gotten over the fact that he cheated, and you stayed. You can't say you forgive someone but punish them. It doesn't work like that. But whatever; that's your business. Have fun."

"Saa—" I paused when she hung up on me. I knew she was mad at me; I just didn't want her jumping down my throat about this shit. I would text her when I got inside of Aminah's house. I hated arguing with my bestie boo. Getting off the elevator, I walked into Minah's apartment, and she was walking toward the door.

"Hey bitch. I was just about to leave," she said, picking up her bag from the floor before giving me a hug. "You look cute too. Please don't go in my bed, cause when Rico and I in town, we do stay here. I will kill you."

"Bitch, don't do me. I am not nasty like that. Plus, I'm not even having sex with him." I rolled my eyes. She balled her face up before chuckling.

"So you cheating on Mack, just not to fuck? Yeah, aight. That's between you, your pussy, and the Man above. Goodbye." She laughed, walking out the door. I didn't know why her and Saaleha were all in my business. Rolling my eyes, I locked the door and took my bag into the guest room before cooking dinner. As soon as dinner was done, my phone rang. Wiping my hands on the rag, I picked it up. It was Mack; my heart started beating fast as I answered.

"Hey babe,"

"What's up, babe? What you doing?" His sexy voice came through the phone, making my heart flutter.

"Nothing. I just got finish cooking us some dinner. Minah in the shower. What you doing?" I partially lied.

"Make sure you bring me a plate when you come home tomorrow. I was just checking on you. I love you, baby." Why he gotta be all nice to me and shit, got me feeling like I'm not shit. But then again, I'm pretty sure I used to call him when he was with a bitch, so whatever.

"I love you more, babe. Kiss Maya for me. I'll see you tomorrow," was all I said. It was good enough for him because we talked for a little longer before we hung up. About ten minutes later, Montez told me he was at the door. Getting my thoughts together, I went to open the door, and I swear the flood gates opened. He stood there looking like a damn entrée. Licking my lips, his eyes flew to them before he checked me out.

"You look good." He bit his bottom lip before he walked into the house, pulling me close to him. "Real good." He crashed his lips against mine, before he inserted his tongue. And baby, I gladly accepted. He picked me up, and my legs unintentionally wrapped around his waist while he carried me over to the sofa.

"Wait, I cooked—" I paused when he kissed me again. This man was about to have me screaming and cumming all over this damn apartment. I felt it; I was way passed horny.

"We can eat after. I want you so bad." He mumbled into my neck before sucking on it. "Let me see something real quick." He pulled away before unbuttoning my pants. He kissed down my stomach, taking my jeans all the way off, before he pulled my panties to the side and dove face first.

"Montezzzzz," I moaned out, gripping the pillows and arching my back. His tongue flicked over my clit a few times, causing my body to go crazy. "Shit, baby," I screamed before I felt myself cumming in his mouth. I had never, and I mean never came this hard from head. See, Mack could do it, but he was not all that. Montez was officially the best I ever had when it came to head.

"Damn, already?" He mumbled into my flower before he kissed it, making my body shiver. This nigga was the truth. He came up kissing me on the lips, before I sucked on his bottom lip. "Let me make love to you, Reds."

Nodding my head, I attacked his lips while pointing at the room. He carried me back there while gripping my ass and kissing all over my neck. Throwing me on the bed, I watched him get undressed while I took my shirt off. When my eyes finally landed back on him, baby was hung like a fucking horse. His dick had to be the same size as Macion's but fatter. My mouth dropped open, causing a smirk to form on his sexy ass face. Like, I had never seen a dick prettier than Macion's. It was a little darker than his light skin tone, and I could see the veins in them. I swear my mouth watered. He walked over to me with his dick swinging, and smiling like he was about to fuck up my life. Climbing over me, he kissed my lips passionately, while rolling the condom that I didn't even know he had, down on his dick.

"You ready?" he asked before his big, flat pink tongue brushed across his bottom lip. I was scared to answer because I couldn't believe I was doing this. So instead of answering, I wrapped my arms around his neck and pulled him close to me.

"Make love to me," was all I whispered before connecting our lips. He inserted inside with me with a little struggle. "Fuck," I moaned.

"Come on, let me in," he groaned inside of my neck. Relaxing my body, I did as I was asked and let him fully in. "Damn," he mumbled. My eyes slammed shut as the feeling took over my body. I couldn't believe this was happening. I was officially a cheater. As much as I wanted to stop, it was no backing out now. "Open your eyes, Reds."

Opening my eyes, I stared into his intense ones. The way he was making me feel right now was indescribable. His strokes deepened as my nails dug into his back, arching my back at the feel of him right on my g-spot. "Mm," I moaned softly before looking off, only for him to grab my face and make me look at him again.

"Keep your eyes on me," he demanded before leaning in for a kiss. As we kissed, his strokes picked up, hammering onto my g-spot. "You better not cum. You cum when I say so, okay?" he said once he pulled away, wrapping my legs around his neck as he watched himself disappear inside of me. "Your pussy shouldn't be this good, yo." He chuckled, bringing a smile to my face because his smile was perfect.

"Baby, wait." I placed my hands onto his stomach to push him away, but he smacked them down. "Fuckkkkk!" I yelled out as I came hard.

"Did I tell you to cum?"

"Montez!" I yelped when he slipped out of me and flipped me over, inserting me from the back.

"Arch it," he whispered into my ear, while I did as I was told. His hands gripped my sides as I started to throw it back on him, matching his long strokes. "Do that shit, baby," he groaned before he slapped my ass to make it jiggle.

"Fuck this pussy, baby!" I yelled out, shocking the hell out of myself, but shit, this dick was lethal, and I wanted it every second of the day. Montez reached his hand around and played with my clit, before his hand wrapped around my neck and his lips connected with my lips.

"Cum with me, baby," he whispered on my lips before he did something I had never had done to me in my life. He pulled away a little, deepening his strokes, and with his hands still wrapped around my neck, he spit in my mouth. "Shit," he groaned as we both came hard, as if that was the best nut of our lives. He slid out of me a little before he collapsed on the bed. We laid there for a little, getting our breathing together. I couldn't believe what just happened, but baby, that shit was one for the books.

"I'm in trouble now." I mumbled, making him chuckle. He leaned up and kissed me on my lips softly.

"Yeah, you are. Now you fucking two shooters." He smirked before he got up to get a rag to clean us up. He was right. I was now fucking two shooters, and it was no backing out now. What was done was done. Maybe I'd cut him off. But then that wasn't fair to me, because I knew I would be addicted to this man. *What did you just do, Amber?*

"So how was it?" Saaleha asked me as she sat in her office behind her desk. She hadn't been talking to me since the other day. I'd been blowing her ass up, and the first day I saw her, she wanted to be reminding me of my weekend with Montez. I had just gotten to work but wanted to see her first because I needed to know if she was still mad at me; seemed as though she was not. Sucking my teeth, I took a seat in front of her desk and stared at her. "I don't know why you are staring at me and shit. I know you fucked him. I know my best friend. So like I said, how was it? He looks like he carries it very well."

Chuckling, I shook my head before speaking. "Lee, I'm in so much trouble. His dick was too damn good. I was hoping it was going to be corny. But bitch, I turned my one night into a weekend thing with him. I'm in so much trouble, I can just feel it."

"Yeah bitch, you are. I tried to warn you! You were better off cheating with a damn lawyer, doctor, or regular ass Philly nigga. Not another shooter, bitch. You gon' die," she dramatically said, making me roll my eyes.

"Crazy thing is, Tez said the same thing. After we were finished on Friday, I told him that I was in trouble, and he said yeah, I am, because I'm fucking two shooters."

"Yeah. Duh, bitch, 'cause if Tez buss, Mack definitely bussing back." She cracked as if this was a good time for her to be cracking jokes. She must've seen my face because she laughed harder. "Oh, you mad? I don't care. You weren't mad when you were talking all that hot shit to me."

"I told you I was sorry like a million times. I was just saying, just like you were."

Different Sides Of The Game 2

"It wasn't about me though; it was about you. My situation is way different from yours, Amber. I'm married and have a child with one man who I thought was dead for five years, while I'm pregnant and in love with another man. My shit needs Iyanla so she can fix my life. You don't need Iyanla; you need to learn how to forgive your daughter's dad." She paused before grabbing my hand. "Just how I said before, Reds, you can't blame him for things you've taken him back for. Cherelle wasn't the first girl he stepped out on you for, she was just the last girl. You can't keep saying to him, 'oh, baby, I forgive you', then turn around and throw it up in his face. It—"

"I haven't thrown it back in his face!" I interrupted, forcing a small chuckle out of her. Shaking her head, she removed her hand from mine and sat back in the chair.

"Having sex Montez is throwing it back in his face. You're messing with Tez because you want Macion to know how it feels to be in your shoes for once. Lowkey, you're probably praying he finds out just, so you can say 'now you know how it feels'. That's throwing it back in his face. But you gotta ask yourself this: When it all comes down to it, is Macion going to take you back? Just because you took him back all those times, doesn't mean he's going to take you back this one time." She read me. My best friend really knew me more than I knew myself sometimes. She was absolutely right though. I didn't think this situation all the way through. I was just using Tez as a distraction, but I fucked up when I allowed him between my legs. If Macion ever found out I gave his pussy away, he would never forgive me. I just knew he wouldn't. *Damn, Amber.*

Macion "Mack" Dupree

Suspicions

Amber had been acting real weird lately. She'd been spending a lot of time with Saaleha and Minah. I wasn't tripping over that, but after that weekend she spent at Minah's house, she came home being extra friendly. Like trying to spend all day with me and shit. Amber hadn't asked to run around with me since she was like twenty-two. Whenever she wasn't at work nowadays, she was with me and getting on my last damn nerves. Then on top of it all, she kept talking about opening an accounting firm. I mean, I knew that was always her dreams, but she was a mom now. She acted like I wasn't going to take care of her. She was already Saaleha's partner down at the glam shop. That was enough in my opinion. But anyway, I had to lock her ass out the baby's room last night because she kept trying to do it to me. I took my ass right to sleep in my daughter's room. I didn't have time for Reds trying to rape me and shit.

Getting up from the beanbag inside of my daughters room, I checked on her, and she was still sound asleep. She was so perfect, and her sleep schedule was great. Reds didn't play that shit. Opening the door, I shook my head at this damn fool sleep on the floor in front of the door. I should have left her ass there, but I didn't feel like fighting her Rambo ass later because I left her there. Bending down, I picked her up and walked her to our bedroom, laying her in bed. She stirred but didn't wake up. I started to walk away before her phone went off. I tried to unlock it, but her password was changed.

Tapping her, she groaned before opening those pretty eyes then looked up at me. "Why you change your password?" I asked. I wasn't insecure or anything, but I knew whenever I changed my password, I was fucking with another bitch.

"Saaleha and Minah be all in my phone, so I changed it," she said, but I knew she was lying. I knew when Amber lied, she never could make eye contact. She would always look off to the side and shit. Nodding my head, I chuckled before placing her phone back on the nightstand. "Why you didn't sleep with me last night?" She changed the subject.

"'Cause you keep trying to rape me and shit." I kissed her forehead before walking into the bathroom. I really didn't want to believe my girl was cheating on me, but I couldn't help this feeling I was getting. I knew she was. I just knew my girl. She got clingy as hell when she did something wrong. Not only was she clingy lately, she'd been trying to have sex more than our usual. Like, don't get me wrong, I liked that shit, but a nigga be needing some sleep. She'd just been moving funny to me. Like, Reds never stayed the weekend out. Maybe a day, but a weekend? Nah, she'd be calling me to come get her or telling me she on her way home. So all this new staying out she'd been doing was raising all red flags. On my momma, I would shoot up anybody who called themselves messing with mine.

Once I got out the shower, I walked back into the bedroom, and Reds was gone with her phone. Shaking my head, I got dressed so I could go meet up with Meen, Jay, and True. Speaking of Meen and True, it seemed as if those niggas loved sharing women. How they both messed with Kristina's crazy ass? Didn't they know that mami's were crazy? Meen loved Hispanic chicks ever since he found out Saaleha was mixed with Dominican. Anyway, I went downstairs and was greeted by the smell of breakfast. Walking into the kitchen, Reds was sitting down, breastfeeding Amaya. That scene alone was just beautiful. I respected the shit out of women for these reasons alone. They were really the beholder of life besides God of course.

"Damn, bae, it smells good." I rubbed my stomach as it growled. She looked over her shoulder and smiled lightly.

"I didn't want my man starving while he's trying to handle his business." Her sneaky ass smiled before getting up and walking over to me. She placed a kiss on my lips then I kissed Amaya's forehead. "How long are you going to be today? I wanted to have date night but somewhere that Maya can come."

"I'm not sure, but I'll let you know, babe. I won't try to be long." My answer must have been good enough for her because she nodded before handing me Maya so that she could make my plate. While she was making my plate, her phone was going off with text messages, but I wasn't going to make a big deal out of it. I'd catch her sneaky ass. I promise I would.

"Yo, I think Reds cheating on me," I said to Meen and Jay, making them look at me like I was crazy. I wanted to bring it up to them before True got here. He was cool and all, but this shit was way past personal for me.

"Reds? As in Amber? Cheating on you, bro?" Meen asked as if he was in shock. Shit, I didn't know why he was in shock. Bitches that constantly got cheated on, finally cheated back one day. I didn't care what nobody said; women cheated better than niggas do.

"Naw, for real, bro; you bugging. Reds would never cheat on you," Jay chimed in.

"Why wouldn't she? I mean, I cheated on her ass since she was a kid. She probably trying to get me back. Man, I know what I feel, and I feel like my bitch cheating." I sucked my teeth, taking a seat at the table inside the warehouse we were at. They both stared at me as if I lost my mind or something. Jay shook his head before he drank some of his soda.

"So tell us why your paranoid ass thinks she is cheating?" Jay folded his arms and stared at me.

Taking a deep breath because I knew these niggas were going to make a joke out of this shit, I said, "Because she's been clingy as fuck, then she's always trying to fuck me. Like, don't get me wrong, Reds and I have sex at least four times a day, sometimes five if Maya sleeping. But lately, she's been trying to be on my dick twenty-four seven, yo."

"She cheating 'cause she horny? You dead ass right now? Bro, you bugging!" Meen said through laughter. I saw they took my life as a joke.

"And she changed the password to her phone," I said, ceasing all the laughing these clowns were doing. Jay sat up straight before cocking his head to the side.

"Well did you ask her why?" Jay asked, and I nodded my head 'yes'. "And what did she say?"

"That Lee and Minah was all in her phone one day, so she changed it. Then that shit was going off all morning, and when I asked her who it was, her thot ass going to say group message." I shook my head when they both gasped.

"Damn, bro. She's cheating, cheating. You know that group message shit is for niggas," Meen said, shaking his head before tugging on his beard. "Not Reds. I don't want that shit to be true."

"I don't either, bro. I wonder who she's messing with?" Jay inquired.

"No cap, 'cause when I find out, I'm putting a bullet right between his eyes, and that shit gon' be on her hands," I barked, just thinking if my shawty was cheating or not.

"Then again, bro, you done cheated on her ass so many times, you really can't be mad." Jay shrugged his shoulders. Meen snapped his head, giving him that 'nigga, really?' look. "What? I'm just saying, fuck he going to do? Leave her? Yeah, aight."

"I don't give a fuck what I did in the past, you don't give a nigga pussy away, bro. Women never cheat how we do. Like, we can have sex with a chick and go back home to wifey unbothered. Women cheat, they all emotionally, physically, and mentally involved. It's deeper than sex when women cheat, man. If she's cheating on me, I know Amber, and I know I won't be able to forgive her." I stressed just thinking about that shit. I prayed to the Most High that she wasn't cheating on me.

"She's probably not even cheating; you just being a dub," Meen assured.

"Naw, bro, that's cap. She's definitely cheating on you, but with who is the question." Jay chimed in, and he was right. I knew my gut, and I trusted my gut always. Amber was cheating on me for sure, and

I couldn't wait until I got to the bottom of this. She was going to wish she never even texted another nigga.

Ahmeen Santana

True Love Never Dies

"What your hoe ass doing?" I smiled into the phone when I heard her suck her teeth. It was crazy how after all these years, no matter what we'd been through, or what I put us through; my love for her has never changed. I just hoped hers didn't.

"Minding my damn business. What your shrimp dick having ass doing?" she cracked back, now it was my turn to suck my teeth. "Ah ha, shrimp dick," she joked into the phone all dumb.

"Yeah, okay. You be the main person screaming and crying that I'm too deep." Yeah, now all that laughing stopped. "I can't wait until you have your baby so I can shoot the club up again."

"What Blueface baby say? Yeah, aight. You not shooting shit up over here."

"So you don't want to have another baby by me, Pocahontas?" I asked her, knowing she wouldn't answer the question. Ever since that day at her mom's house, we'd been getting along, spending family time together and everything. I was happy as hell that she was allowing me around her and my son. She wasn't lying when she said she wanted me around them; her ass be calling me for everything whenever True ain't around.

"Whatever. When are you bringing my son home, Meenie?" I could just tell by her voice that she was smiling. She never cared how much I hated that name; she still called me it. "Ahmeen!"

"Shut up with all that yelling. I'm about to bring him there now. Cool out." We talked on the phone for a little until I picked Lil' Meen up from Kaylina's house. Then we had to hang up because I was being 'nasty', Saaleha said.

I had just pulled up to Saaleha's house, bringing Lil' Meen back home from our weekend together. Since it was her birthday, I decided to allow her to have some relaxing time since she couldn't really do shit since she was pregnant. It felt good to be around my son again, even if his mom was a dub. I still missed these times. And what made it better was this go 'round, I was able to give him my undivided attention because I wasn't in the streets no more. All my shit was behind the scenes, except this shit with Kristina and Kiera. Oh, I was definitely getting my hands dirty for them. Walking up to the door, I punched the door code in before allowing Lil' Meen and myself inside. As soon as we walked in the door, we were hit by the smell of food. Taking our shoes off, Lil' Meen ran to the kitchen with me right behind him.

"Mom!" Lil' Meen yelled before hugging Saaleha. She smiled, hugging him back.

"How was your weekend with dad?" she asked while he took a seat at the island. Her eyes flew over to me, and her bottom lip went in between her teeth, as she looked me up and down. She was still feeling the kid no matter how much she fronted. Her eyes traveled back to my face before she nodded in approval, making me chuckle.

"It was so much fun. We went shopping in New York, and I got some more games. Dad brought me an Xbox One S for his house." He smiled brightly. Saaleha's head snapped my way. She hated when I spoiled him as if she didn't do the same. Shrugging my shoulders, I pulled out my phone, scrolling through my unread text messages.

"Go get cleaned up for dinner," Saaleha said to Lil' Meen. Doing as he was told, he left out the kitchen, leaving us alone. "Do you want to stay for dinner?"

"How your boy going to feel about that?" I smirked, making her roll her eyes. Sucking her teeth, she threw her middle finger up.

"Coming from the nigga who always throw out that we're still married." She sucked her teeth, causing me to laugh. "But, I'm single—"

"You're still married," I cut her off, making her laugh before shaking her head. "Nah, but I'll stay. Shit, you know I love your cooking."

We did what we'd been doing since I'd been back: we had family dinner. I knew Saaleha hadn't forgiven me yet, but I knew she would. I wouldn't stop trying with her stubborn ass if it was the last thing I did. After dinner, Lil' Meen went upstairs to play his game and talk to Kaylina. My little nigga was a ladies' man, just like his pops. After Lee and I finished cleaning up the kitchen like old times, she went to go lay on the sofa with her feet up. Walking over to the sofa, I sat down next to her, sucking my teeth. She loved reality shows. But I wasn't going to say nothing though, 'cause *Black Ink Crew* was my shit too. That girl Sky, man, she was bad as shit; ratchet, but fine as hell. Picking up Saaleha's feet, I instantly started to massage them.

"You always gave the best foot massages." She practically moaned, bringing a laugh out of me.

"And you always moaned during them, freak ass." Saaleha burst out laughing before shaking her head. She knew I was right. She always said I was really good with my hands and always made her body feel good. "What's up with your hair?"

"Don't do me. Can you straighten it for me though?" She pouted, making me suck my teeth. "Meenie, you used to do it for me all the time, come on!" She whined, making me chuckle. She got up and ran to get the bumpers and came back down.

"You really be having me do some nut shit. Do your corny ass baby dad do this shit?" I asked as she smiled brightly, sitting on the sofa after she plugged the bumpers in.

"No. I didn't feel like teaching him how I taught you." She smirked, making me laugh. She taught me how to do her hair when she was pregnant. I wasn't no pro or shit, but I got her little hair straightened. Talking about if we have a daughter one day, I needed to know how to do it.

"So how was your weekend?" I asked as I took a deep breath. She really could make me do anything.

"I spent it with Amber and my god baby. I can't believe her crazy ass is a mom."

"Naw, forreal. Like, Reds a mom. I pray for my niece, man." I chuckled. "She already talking about beating Kiera up." Reds been blowing my phone up saying how she wanted to fight Kiera and everything, getting on my damn nerves.

"Oh, I know. That's all her and Minah talking about. Speaking of that bitch, what are you planning to do?" Saaleha asked.

"That's none of your—"

"Ahmeen, I'm not about to go no more years without you. It's my business, you're my business. We still married, remember? And that little nigga back there that looks just like you, deserves to have you in his life. So I deserve to know everything. So start fucking talking," she demanded.

"Lee, I'm going to handle that shit. And when I get her, I promise to call you. You're going to be there. I'm not going to leave you out of shit else," I said while placing the bumpers down and making her face me. "And stop talking to me like I'm some nut ass nigga too. I've been letting you slide, but you getting too carried away. Fix that shit before I fix it for you. I'm not that nigga True. I'll choke your dumb ass out."

Her mouth fell open as she stared at me, before she bit her bottom lip. Freak ass. I wasn't playing with her either. She'd been getting a little to beside herself, talking to me like I was anybody. I wasn't with that shit. I get she was mad and shit, but that didn't mean she could disrespect me. I wasn't with that shit before. I didn't know why she would think I was with it now.

"Whatever, Ahmeen. I'm just saying I'm not trying to live without you again! I went crazy," she mumbled before pouting with her punk ass. I placed the straighteners down on the table, because I didn't even feel like doing her hair in the first place. Taking a seat next to her, I picked her feet up again and put them in my lap.

"Whatever my ass. I don't care what you talking about. Stop disrespecting me. I'm trying here. I'm trying real hard to fix this shit, but one day you act like you going to let me back in, then the next you back on that bullshit. Like what's really—"

"I'm working it out with True," she blurted out. Nodding my head, I removed her feet from my lap before I stood up. Walking in front of her, I saw her body tense up completely; her ass was bluffing. Bending down in front of her, I stared in her eyes; well, I tried too. She wouldn't look me in the eyes.

"Divorce me then," I spoke calmly.

"Wh-what?" she stuttered.

"Since you've found out I was still alive, Pocahontas, you haven't asked me for a divorce. You know that one day that nigga going to want to marry you, but you can't 'cause you're still married to me."

"I'm a wid—"

"I'm still alive. Saaleha, stop fighting me. Let me make this right; we're married. We said death do us part, ma. Even after death. Give me a chance," I pleaded with her. I didn't give a damn how I looked or how I sounded. I needed my wife back.

"I'm having a baby with True," she reasoned.

"And? We have a son! Stop making excuses. You love me, Saaleha. I'm the love of your life; don't fight it," I stated softly, making her look away. "Come on, man. I love the shit out of you. I never stopped. I get it, I fucked up, but I did what I had to do for my family, Lee. You can't fault me for that. I've given you time. Take me back ma, please."

"I can't do that to him. I love him, Ahmeen."

"Divorce me then," I said again, making her bite down on her lip. She shook her head in disbelief. "Just think about it, Lee. We weren't just dating, Lee. You don't just give up on your marriage no matter how hard shit gets." I kissed her lips before I walked away from her, leaving her stuck. I put myself out there for her. I get what's going on with her, but she had to be real with me, real with True, and real with herself. Because, *true love never dies*, for real.

Few Days Later...

"What's wrong with you?" I asked True when he walked into the building that I'd been working on opening for my tattoo shop with Jay. Jay and I had been planning on opening this tattoo shop since we were kids, but when they tried to kill me, it got pushed back. Now that I was back, we were hype as shit to get it open. True sucked his teeth before taking a seat on the chair in the lobby part.

"How do you deal with Saaleha ass? Man, she been giving me the cold shoulder for a couple weeks, man. I tried to do something with her for her birthday; she just wanted her gifts. Talking about she needs her, '*me*', time. The fuck is that?" I wanted to burst out laughing, but I knew his pain. Saaleha was stubborn as hell.

"That's my wife for you, but she's stubborn, bro. I'm pretty sure you know that, especially when she's pregnant. What she like six or seven months?"

"Six almost seven."

"Yeah, give her time; that's all I can say." I shrugged my shoulders. "But, on another note, have you been in contact with Kristina?"

"No. She's been laying low. I think she went back out to Mexico. But I killed one of her men the other—"

"Nigga, what? Why?" I interrupted him. *His ass gotta be crazy*, I thought to myself shaking my head. He shrugged his shoulders before laughing.

"He was following me around and shit. He should've been more discreet. I took his ass right to the warehouse and ended it all for him. So she'll be back soon. Trust me."

"You crazier than me, nigga." I chuckled, shaking my head. "I know that's not all you came over here for. So what's good?"

"Kristina's dad called me the other day, threatening me because I choked his daughter, but also threatened you because you dumped his daughter." He chuckled when I sucked my teeth.

"He doesn't want no smoke with me. I'm not worried about his old ass. I fear his psycho ass daughter before I allow him to pump fear in my blood." I never was afraid of going against anybody in any cartel because we all bled the same blood. Plus, just how them niggas had pull, so did I, sometimes from people in their own crew.

"You right, he doesn't. He just wants us to apologize to her. I tried to apologize to her, but all she told me was fuck me and to watch my back. And Saaleha's back." When he brought up Saa's name, my jaw tightened. I didn't know why Kristina kept bringing Saaleha up and why she kept threatening her, but I was about to put an end to all of it.

"Bet. We going to be paying her a visit real soon. For sure." It was about to get real dark, not only for Kiera, but for Kristina too.

Kiera Mitchell

My Truth

♡

I was fourteen years old, and my mom, Keisha, had sent me out to New York to stay with my father, Kenny, for the summer. I hated it because I would be away from Saa and Amber, but this was my normal ever since they had gotten a divorce. We used to be the perfect family. My father worked downtown as an accountant, and my mother was a nurse. I admired my parents' relationship and their career paths because, unlike my two best friends, we lived in a residential area in Ardmore. I lived a high sadity life—tennis practices, play dates, and everything. I always thought things were going great, but boy was I wrong. My mom met a man… Rodney, that was his name. I'd never forget his name because he ruined my life. He introduced my mother to heroin. She would come home late, and they would argue, forcing my father to stay in the guest room. Then they would put on friendly faces in the morning. I guess to protect me. But I'd always remember the arguments.

Months went on and my mother had gotten worse. No matter how many times I heard my dad say he would leave her, that wasn't enough to stop her. Now, she was in love with Rodney, who supposedly gave her a new feel. When she told my dad that, it broke him. I saw him break, and I was pissed at her for that. Even though he was hurt, he stayed; he loved my mom. I could always tell. But that love wasn't enough for Keisha, because she stayed on drugs and stayed with Rodney. She stopped coming home some nights, and my dad ended up moving us to New York when I was nine. That forced my mom to get clean, well, pretend she was. I went back to Philly when I was eleven and picked up my life, and so did my mom. We had to downgrade our life tremendously. We moved to Overbrook, from a four bedroom, to a two-bedroom apartment. I loved living in

West Philly because I was close to my two best friends. My mom lost her job and refused to allow my dad to help us. When my mom got back on drugs, she begged me to not tell my dad. She said she'd let me do whatever I wanted and buy me whatever I wanted. So I protected my mom, knowing I should've just told my dad she needed help.

Since they were always worried about my mom, they never focused on me. They never focused on what I was going through; they were never worried about the young me. Nobody knew what I had to endure in life; nobody knew why I was the way I was, nor did they try to find out. I was never good enough for nobody, not even my mom. So I picked up this lifestyle I lived at the age of fourteen, and hadn't looked back since. It all started when I spent one summer with my dad and his new family.

I had just got off Amtrak train at the Grand Central Terminal. When I came up the steps, I was greeted by my dad, his new wife, Linda, and her son, Lamont. I actually liked Linda; she was very motherly, which wasn't something I was getting at home at the time. When I first met Linda, I didn't really like her, but I guess I had to get used to her, because now, I loved her as if she was my own mother.

"Hey, baby girl," my father said, pulling me into a tight hug, forcing a smile out of me. I was such a daddy's girl. Even though I looked exactly like my mom, I had my father's eyes, nose, and caramel complexion.

"You're suffocating her, Kenny!" Linda said, making me chuckle. She was right, he was, but I was used to it. My dad let me go, then Linda pulled me into her, not even giving me a chance to take a breath. "We missed you so much!"

"I missed y'all more." I chuckled, enjoying the motherly hug. I don't even know the last time my mother hugged me or even told me she loved me.

Pulling away from the embrace with Linda, I looked over at Lamont, who was biting his bottom lip at me. Lamont was seventeen at the moment. He creeped me out in so many ways. It wasn't like he wasn't attractive; he was deep chocolate, stood about five feet ten, had a curly top that was tapered on the sides, and he could've been any girl's dream guy. But to me, he was just weird. I caught him watching me a few times, but I never paid it no mind, because he's supposed to be my stepbrother. Anyway, we stared at each other before he reached his arms out as if he was asking for a hug, then walked toward me. He pulled me in a tight hug just as my dad and Linda did.

"I missed you, sis." He whispered in my ear before I felt his lips touch my neck, causing me to jump back. He let me go from his tight embrace, offering a big smile, then grabbed my duffle bag out of my hand. Looking over at my dad and Linda, who missed that whole encounter, I took a deep breath before we walked out the train station. I wasn't going to make a big deal out of it. He probably didn't even mean it in a sexual way. I hoped not.

Weeks went by, and as always, I loved being in New York. Even though I missed Saaleha and Amber so much, we talked on three-way every single night. I was enrolled in a summer dance program, which I enjoyed the most. My goal was to enroll in Juilliard one day. Anyway, I was chilling in my room that Linda had decorated for me; everything was pretty in pink. It reminded me of Saaleha's room; well, it was exactly like hers. I sent pictures of her room to Linda. I wasn't no weirdo or nothing like that; I just liked her room a lot. I was scrolling through MySpace at the time, when my bedroom door opened, and Lamont walked in. My eyes traveled to his as he walked over to my bed and sat down.

"What you doing, lil' sis?" He spoke calmly with his back toward me, making me relax again. You never know with him; he was very hot and cold and creeped me out.

"Uh, nothing, just relaxing." I paused when he turned to face me. His eyes were bloodshot red; he looked high to be exact. "Mont, are you okay? You look, uh, a little tired or something."

"Yeah, I'm good. Could you get me some tissue though?" he asked with a small smile. I wanted to get smart and tell him to get that shit himself, but Lamont has always been nice to me besides him being creepy. Nodding my head, I got up, heading to the bathroom in the hall. When I made it back to my room, Lamont wasn't there anymore. Then my door slammed shut, forcing me to jump. Turning around, he was standing behind my door, licking his lips.

"Wh-what are you doing?" I stuttered, backing into the corner of my room trying to get away from him. He didn't say a word as he followed my steps, just staring at me and lusting over me. "Lamont, what's—"

Different Sides Of The Game 2

"Just shut up. You need to calm down. Here, take this!" He yelled, making me flinch at the deepness of his voice. His hand opened and he had two pills. I shook my head, and he chuckled before pushing me against the wall.

"Why are you doing this, Lamont?" I stood in the corner of my bedroom while he gripped my face and forced those pills down my throat. He stared at me while holding me against the wall.

"You don't trust me, lil' sis?" Lamont asked before a soft smile graced his face and his hands glided up and down my frame. I stood in the corner with a pair of Juicy Couture shorts on, and a tank top. Even at fourteen, I had a nice body after I hit puberty, of course. His hands gripped my butt, making me flinch, before his lips glided across my face then my neck. "Come on, I won't hurt you. Just come on."

Lamont spun on his heels, while grabbing my arm, basically dragging me with him. Our parents were out having a date night, so it was just Lamont and I in the house. I had never wished my dad was around so bad, until now. I was starting to feel the effects of whatever I took, as we walked through the three-bedroom home until we got down to the basement. Reaching the basement, we were greeted by two of Lamont's friends. I stopped in my tracks, making Lamont turn to face me. I'd seen his friends before; they were weird to me too. They always lusted after me, but I would always brush it off.

"You trust me?" was all he asked before his two friends walked toward me. I tried to back away, but Lamont grabbed my hair, forcing me to stay in position. "Stay still; they not going to hurt you!"

"Please, no! Lamont! Please, no!" My pleas fell deaf to his ears, as his friends got closer to me. "Lamont, please." I cried.

"She's a virgin, so that's two hundred dollars per person. If you want her to suck your dick, that's an extra fifty dollars," Lamont said, making my eyes widen. He was pimping me out. I couldn't believe my own stepbrother was pimping me out.

"How can you do this? Lamont, please, no. I won't say anything, just let me go," I cried, trying to push him off me, but that only angered him more.

"Bitch, shut up! You not my real sister. You fine and all. I think I'm going to fuck first, break this virginity in. Then y'all can have her, still for a fee though." He chuckled before he pulled me against him, placing his hard dick onto my butt. "Matter fact, I can make your first time special. Let's go in my

Page | 155

bedroom." *He kissed my lips before dragging me to his room. I cried the whole way, but it didn't matter. He still took my innocence and still allowed his friends to have their way with me. For the rest of the summer, this was an everyday thing. Eventually, I got used to it and addicted to those pills that he would give to me every time before I had a client. Until I was able to tell my parents, that I didn't want to go to New York any longer, every summer, all the way to the age of eighteen, he pimped me out, and eventually we just started fucking each other all the time. He ruined me, and nobody did a damn thing to stop it. That was just the beginning of Kiera, and I have no remorse for anything or anyone.*

Khyreema Jenkins

Everything great comes to an end.

"Baby." I heard Jayceon mumble before I felt him nudge me. Then I felt his lips on my face repeatedly. "Khy baby, wake up," he said again before running his hand over my stomach and pulling me back toward him.

"Not yet. Ten more minutes." I groaned while burying my head into the pillow, I was sleeping so well, like I always did when I was in bed with him. I had spent the night with him, while Dani babysat Kaylina for me. It was nice to have a night off and just be under my man.

"No. Come on, it's almost eight p.m. I know Kay misses you." He kissed my face before he climbed out of bed. I watched my man stand there naked as the day he was born. Listen, Jayceon was so perfect; his body was sculpted so nicely due to him always being in the gym. His arms were the perfect size, like not too small but not super big; they were just right. His six pack was just everything. I loved running my tongue across them. He was just so manly. I loved everything about him. I was so lucky.

"Stop staring at a nigga like you want to eat me." He smirked before making his member jump. "You not getting no dick either; come on. I got shit to do. I been laying in bed with your ass all day. Let's go," he demanded, making me suck my teeth, but he was right. I needed to get home to my baby.

After I got out of bed, we took a shower, and of course I got some dick, so it took us a little longer. After we finished washing up and getting dressed, I made him drive all the way to King of Prussia for California Pizza Kitchen so I could get something to eat for my little family. I was surprised Danielle or Diamond didn't call me yet. Kay must've been being good today. Her ass been acting up lately. As we drove, we held hands. Jayceon was it for me, I swear. I felt it. I loved this man's cockiness, loved how arrogant he was, and loved how passionate he was about things he loved. He was just what I was missing all my life and all that me and Kaylina needed.

"Babe, I have something to tell you," I stated, going into my purse. I wanted to tell him when the time was right, but I couldn't wait any longer.

"What's good?" he asked before looking over at me when we got to a light. I held the pregnancy test in my hand, and I swear my heart jumped for joy when I saw the tears forming in his tough ass eyes. I made a gangsta cry, y'all. "You dead ass? Like you dead ass carrying my seed, baby?" He smiled as he whipped the car over and placed it in park.

"Yes, we're having a baby! I found out last night. I wanted to do something special, but I was too excited. Baby, we're about to be a complete family," I raved.

"Yo, if I could fall deeper in love with you, Khy baby, this would be the moment. Damn, you about to have a nigga baby." He kissed my lips.

His happiness was all I needed. I remembered when I found out I was pregnant with Kaylina. Neither Malcolm or I was this happy. Of course, I loved my baby, but I was a kid who had no idea what it meant to be a mom, and this time around, I felt like I was not putting my kid in the middle of my bullshit. I had no doubts or regrets when it came to Jayceon. We sat in that spot, just talking, before he finished driving me home. Pulling up to the house, he grabbed my hand and kissed the back of it.

"I love you. I think you should let Dani and Diamond have this house, then you and Kay move in with me so we can be a complete family," he suggested. I was so with that. I needed to wake up to my man every single day, with my daughter right in the same household. It was already perfect because Kay loved her Jay Jay as if he was her father, and he loved his Kay Kay like she was his first born.

"I think that's a great idea, babe. I love you, too." I placed a soft kiss on his lips before getting out the car. I was on cloud nine. Nothing, and I mean nothing could ruin this for me. When I walked inside the house, I did not expect it to be dark; they must've been upstairs.

"Familyyyyy, I have some good news," I sang as I turned on the light, jumping back at the person who was sitting on the steps. "Wh-what are you doing here?" I stuttered, asking Malcolm. He was sitting on the steps with Kaylina in his lap with a gun in his hand. Looking to my right, I noticed Danielle and Diamond were tied up in a chair, crying with duct tape over their mouths. It was like I instantly started to cry. This shit was all my fault. I should've killed this nigga when I had the chance.

"You know, Khyreema. I thought I made myself clear that if you ever left me, I would kill you. But you and my dumb ass ex-wife thought it would be cool to run away from me, taking my fucking daughters!" he barked out, making me flinch. I made eye contact with my Kaylina, who was so confused and scared.

"Please let her go. Please, Malcolm. You're scaring her," I begged. Whenever Kaylina would get scared, she'd freeze up. She wouldn't say a word, she would just freeze. It was something I picked up from her when she was five years old. Whenever Kay thought she was going to get in trouble for acting up in school, she would do this.

"Why is my own fucking daughter scared of me? Oh, I know why. Because her dumb ass momma kept her away from me!" he yelled but let Kaylina go, and she darted toward me. Picking her up, I looked over at Dani and Diamond, allowing the tears to cascade down my face. This shit really was all my damn fault.
"Malcolm, untie them, please?" I asked softly, while he rubbed the gun against his temple and sighed deeply.

"I'll untie them if you pack up you and Kaylina's shit and leave with me."

"Malcolm, why? Please, I don't—"

"You love me, that's why! I'm not fucking playing with you, Khyreema. Get your shit and let's go! Or I'll kill Dani," he barked out, causing me to cry harder. Looking over at Dani again, she was shaking her head no. Malcolm snatched the tape off her mouth and placed the gun to Danielle's head. "I'll kill her ass right now!"

"No, Khy, don't go with him! Think about Kaylina," Danielle cried.

"Danielle, are you crazy? No, I'm just going to go. You have a child too, remember?" I said before setting Kaylina on her feet. "I'll just go with you now; it's no need to pack. Just untie them, Malcolm. Please," I begged.

"No, go pack first. We need to get out of here, so hurry up!" he barked. I prayed to God that Jayceon came back here just because. I prayed that he felt my energy and that I was not okay. I needed Jayceon more than ever. I did not want to go with Malcolm.

Please God, if you're listening, watch over us and send Jayceon a sign that I am not okay. Amen.

Amber "Reds" Wright

Who you rocking with?

I swear Macion knew that I was cheating on him. I just knew he did. He was always asking questions and shit, knowing damn well I didn't know how to lie. I be trying to keep up with the lies, but his ass was nosey, okay! Then it didn't make it no better because now Montez was demanding time, more time that I didn't have to spare because I was not trying to die and shit. Nobody cared about me though. I was in a relationship with two shooters, that both been threatening to kill me if I played with either one of them. Then on top of that, Minah and Lee just thought this shit was so damn funny, but it was okay, because they were going to be the main ones crying at my funeral. I was just praying I wouldn't get caught up, because honey, I did not have time to be fighting two grown ass men. I was crazy, but not that damn crazy.

Anyway, I had just got to New York to pop up on Montez. He'd been ignoring me for days now. Even though I missed him, I think I was just going to end it today, because I couldn't risk losing Mack. What Saaleha said was true. Just because I was getting him back for what he did to me, didn't mean that he would be as forgiving as me. So, my best bet was to end it with Tez's fine ass, and goodness, I was not ready to give up all that fineness. Shooting him a text, I let him know that I was here before grabbing my things and headed upstairs. I couldn't believe this nigga got me traveling for him, like it's just New York, but I knew if he was still living in Florida, my ass would've been on any flight for him. That's how much I was feeling him, so I knew this shit was about to be hard.

When I made it to the door, my panties instantly got wet from this nigga. He opened the door in a pair of shorts with those tights thingies underneath. He didn't have a shirt on and his chest was glistening with sweat. Looking back up at his face, he wore a deep frown, making me sigh deeply. We'd been going back and forth for days now, mainly because I felt myself falling for him and I knew I was going to get caught up. Sucking his teeth, he grabbed my bag out my hand and walked away from the door. I smirked a little because I knew he wouldn't have turned me away. Following him into the kitchen, I looked around. His condo was nice as hell. He had tall windows with the view of the city. When we got to the kitchen, he set my bag on the counter before walking over to the refrigerator and taking a water out. He downed that water before throwing it in the trash and gave me his undivided attention.

"So, why are you here, Amber?" His deep baritone voiced flowed through the entire kitchen and through my body. *This is your time to shine, Amber. Say something*, I thought to myself as I stared at his fine ass. My eyes traveled to his body and couldn't believe I was tripping off this light-skinned nigga. I needed to get a grip.

"You've been ignoring me, so I decided to come to you." I shrugged before taking a seat on the stool at the island. He stared at me for a little before he shook his head and laughed. "What's funny?"

"You, man." He chuckled before jumping up on the counter. His kitchen was so big, and I was happy we had space between each other, because the way my clit was throbbing right now, baby, I was about to say fuck ending things. "You tell me you are feeling me, you spending time with me, fucking me one minute, then the next you are ignoring a nigga calls and texts like I'm some regular nigga. Now you popping up and shit. This shit is beyond me. Just be real with yourself; this shit ain't going nowhere. It's just sex. So save the extra feelings shit you be spitting and got me on."

My mouth dropped open in complete shock. I couldn't believe he said it was just sex. "You dead ass, Montez? Just sex? Is that what you think of me, just a fuck? I thought we were better than that." I stared at him in utter disbelief. "You gotta understand, I have a daughter, I have a man, I—"

"Yeah, I know, you got a man. We can talk about that shit, 'cause you cheating on him with me! And you can sit there and say whatever you want about us, but you know this shit is just sex. No matter how much I fuck with you, you go home to your man once you leave me, Reds. This shit on you, not me." He interrupted me. His face was red as hell, showing he was pissed, he was over there looking all fucking good. Man, I should've fucked him first before I chose to argue.

"It wasn't supposed to get this deep, Tez! It—"

"How the fuck you going to say it wasn't supposed to get deep when we've been spending all this time together? When I've been fucking you raw, Amber. You let me stick my dick in you raw. You weren't worried about yo' nigga or how deep this shit was getting. You were in the moment, the right moment, because you know just like I know that deep down this is exactly where you want to be!" He barked out, telling me about myself.

He was right.

He was telling me shit that I couldn't even deny; this was exactly where I wanted to be—right here with him, just missing my daughter. But no matter what I wanted, I couldn't leave Macion, I couldn't do that to my daughter. She deserved a two-parent home, something I always wanted.

"Tez, listen, it's—"

"You want a family because you never had one, I know. But that doesn't mean stay with a nigga you not happy with because y'all got history. That nigga didn't know how to treat you your entire life, ma, but you stayed like a weak bitch that I know you're not. You love that nigga, that's no doubt, but you not in love with that nigga, Reds."

"How you going to tell me who I'm in love with?" I scrunched my face up, this nigga bugging. He jumped down off the counter, walking over to me. I felt my body getting hot, and I was nervous as hell. When he got closer, he stood in front of me with his arms folded. His face looked like he was in deep thought.

"Because you in love with me, ma," he said confidently, forcing my head to snap back. He was tripping; I was not in love with him. "Tell me you not."

"I'm not in love with— what are you doing?" I asked when he picked me up, placing me on the counter. Standing in between my legs, he rubbed my thighs up and down before looking me in my eyes.

"I see the way you stare at me when you think I'm not paying attention. You be mad nervous around me, and I always feel the love when I'm around you. Your energy that strong, ma. I don't know, I just know." He shrugged before looking off. "Or maybe I know because everything you feel, I feel the same way."

He put it all out there for me. He was good for me, he believed in me, and he pushed me. Why couldn't I just be with him? Why didn't I have the balls to leave Macion for Montez?

"Man, you got me on some sucka shit, it's what—" I cut him off with a kiss, a deep kiss, because he was right; I was in love with him. Even though I wanted to deny it, I couldn't, because it was real. My feelings for him were beyond real. It was just Macion. I couldn't do that to him.

Pulling away, he stared at me for a little before I spoke. "You're right, I love you. I'm in love with you, and no matter how hard I try to ignore it, I can't fight it. I'm just scared. Mack is all I know. I've been with him since I was fifteen years old, baby. I'm twenty-seven years old. That's a lot of time to be throwing away."

"Don't mistake time for loyalty and love, ma," he said softly.

"I'm not. It's just I have never done no shit like this before. Yeah, whenever we broke up, I would date someone, but never like this. No nigga was ever able to have me open like you, and it scares me. It scares me so bad, because I'm so dependent on Macion that I don't want to ever be this dependent on anyone else," I expressed.

"Since I've known you, I have never asked you to depend on me for shit. I'm the one who been going with you to look at buildings for your accounting firm. Has that nigga even helped?" he asked, making me look down. "Or is he telling you that you don't need to work and just keep working at the shop?"

"Montez—"

"Nah, lil' baby. I want what's best for you, and I'm what's best for you. You know that shit, but I'm not pressuring you into nothing.

You'll see, and when you do, you'll come around. Just hope that I'm still here waiting," was all he said before he placed a wet kiss on my lips and walked out the kitchen, leaving me there to think.

First off, how was he going to tell me he was what's best for me? *His cocky ass*, I thought to myself. I didn't know what to do. I needed to call my best friend; she knew what to do. Pulling out my phone, I started to call Lee before I heard Montez arguing with somebody with a familiar voice. Jumping down off the counter, I rounded the corner and almost shitted a brick. Macion was standing there with his gun drawn and pointed at Montez, while Tez stood there unfazed and chuckling. It was like they both felt me because their eyes flew to me. Montez face held a look that I couldn't make out, while Macion's face held nothing but pain. I knew that look; it was the look I always gave him. I broke his heart. I thought when this time came, I'd be able to talk my shit, but seeing his face right here, right now, I couldn't help the tears flowing out my eyes.

Get me out of this one, God. I'll be good I promise!

Saaleha Santana

Forever Down 4 You.

Things for me had been complicated because I had no clue what I wanted to do. I didn't know if I wanted to just get back with Meen or stay with True. It was like the most complicated thing I ever had to choose from, and I thought finding a nail color was hard. Then on top of that, True had been asking me when I was divorcing Meen. Like, I didn't even know if that was something I wanted to do. It's crazy because, no matter what, I'd always be down for them both, but life didn't work like that. I had to choose. I mean, I would one day, just not today; maybe after my daughter was born. Right now, I needed to focus on myself and my unborn daughter.

"Mom, do you think you and dad will ever get back together?" Lil' Meen asked me as we walked through Target. I loved Target but hated it at the same time. It was so addicting. Like I could never go to Target with a list; Target told me what to get.

"Why? You don't like the little arrangement we have now? What's wrong with True?" I asked as I put more things into my cart. I was shocked that he even brought this up. I swore he was cool with everything.

"Nothing is wrong with True. I like our little blended family. I'm just asking for dad though." He shrugged, making me laugh. I couldn't believe Meen's stupid ass got my son trying to talk me into getting back with him. Lil' Meen wandered off to get some snacks while I stayed in the baby section. I couldn't wait until this little girl came; I was so ready to meet her. As I was looking at some car seats, I noticed two men in all black walking up toward me. Snapping my head in the other direction, it was two more men.

"I wouldn't do that if I was you." I heard Kristina's voice stopping me from grabbing my phone out my purse. "It's so good to see the bitch who took both of my men." Men? The fuck she meant men? "Oh, you didn't know? I've been dating Meen for about three years, sweetie."

See, this nigga had me fucked up.

"What do you want?" I sucked my teeth.

"You to come with me, and before you try to get all tough, remember you're pregnant. Plus, we're the ones with the guns." She smirked before her men grabbed my arms. My eyes traveled to the end of the aisle, where Lil' Meen was standing with his mouth open. When his eyes landed on mine, I nodded my head, forcing him to pull out his phone to call his dad or True. Getting in the car, they blindfolded me; we were driving for about thirty minutes before we pulled up somewhere. I felt them carefully helping me out the truck and walking me into the building. Once they took my blindfolds off, I noticed we were in a warehouse.

Looking around, I saw Kiera standing over with Kristina, talking. This fake ass bitch. I couldn't believe her. "Really, Kee?"

"Aw, look at my bestie. You pregnant again? What are you having this time?" She smiled, walking toward me as if everything was all good. She was truly a psycho; it was no if, ands, buts about it.

"A girl, finally."

"Finally got your Melody Amora." Kiera smirked.

"Why am I here, Kiera? I don't understand."

"Because you're going to die, sis. You really got enemies everywhere. And I couldn't risk my life for you, oh no." She smirked. She was dead ass psycho. I stared at my childhood best friend in complete disbelief. She'd really gone off the deep end. First, she tried to kill Meen, now me? What the fuck did I ever do to her?

"What happened to you, Kee? You were never like this. It was like after the you spent those summers with your dad, you were a whole other person," I questioned softly.

"Oh, now you care?" Kiera angrily chuckled.

"Kiera, what? I've always cared. I noticed the shit. I even asked you, but you brushed it off. Then you started doing fake things to hurt me. Jealous shit—"

"Ain't nobody jealous of you, Saaleha! Get out your own little world. This shit doesn't revolve around you! People go through real shit in real life! What? Your mom put you out, but you still had a rich ass nigga to protect and love you! You didn't go through anything! Amber and I did. Perfect little Saaleha had Ahmeen to fix everything, and that's all you cared about! I'm the one who got sent out New York and pimped out by my own fucking stepbrother and mom eventually, just so she can snort some damn coke! I was robbed my innocence! You think I give a fuck about that shit your nigga gave you. Saaleha, if it wasn't for Ahmeen you would be a fucking nobody! You were a fucking nobody before he came into your life. Get off your high and mighty; the world doesn't fucking revolve around you!" Kiera screamed out with tears flowing down her eyes.

It was crazy how you could know somebody for years and never know what they'd been through. If someone told me that Kiera went through the shit she did, I would've thought they were lying, but sitting here watching my best friend break in front of me, I finally knew why. I just didn't understand what that had to do with me. If anything, I'd been there for her. I would've been there for her.

"Why didn't you say—"

"Say what, huh? You wanted me to come to you and Reds like 'oh, yeah my stepbrother sold my body.' Naw, I wasn't coming like that. Y'all was so blind, and niggas loved y'all without fucking y'all, and here I was, worn the fuck out. So yeah, I did little nut shit to hurt y'all, but y'all never had to—"

"Shut up!" I yelled out with tears flowing down my face. No matter what, Kiera was my best friend, and to know she had to go through something so horrific scared me. "Little shit to hurt us? You took my child's father away from him because of some shit *you* had to endure? You know how many fucking nights I had to tell my son his fucking father was in heaven and he wasn't coming back? When I went through that shit, you remember what you told me? You told me to go see a therapist and get the fuck over it. So here I am telling you to go see a fucking therapist and get the fuck over it. That shit is your stepbrother's fault! It's not your fault, Reds fault, and damn sure not mine! It's not my fault how I was raised, it's not my fault that I met Ahmeen! I'm so fucking sorry you had to go through that. Kiera, we were best friends. I would've done anything in this world for you. I hope everything was worth it," I snapped.

"It was. You felt pain that I felt—" She paused before looking behind me. I already knew who it was, especially when I saw two men drop down next to me, and every other man drop, before I felt Meen and True by my side. "I- you, how are you even here?" Kiera stuttered.

"You worried about the wrong shit, shawty. Next time make sure he does a head shot." Meen's voice dripped with venom. My eyes flew to True who was staring at Kristina as she held a gun facing us with shaky hands.

"Kris, put the gun down," True demanded.

"No! I'm sick of this bitch, just like Kiera is! This bitch comes in and you leave me, this nigga decides to go back to her. No, I'm ending this shit right now. Fuck her, fuck y'all baby. I'm sick of this shit!" Kristina yelled.

"I know you not trying to kill me behind some dick? Sis, you can have the both of them. I'm a mom first. I don't care about the extra shit." I sucked my teeth while True and Meen both stared at me like they were shocked. "What? Nigga, I pick me and my kids over anybody any day."

"Man, Kris, put the gun down before I body you. I was never yours to keep, and neither was True. We both were married when you met us, baby girl. Let that shit go." He paused before cocking his gun back at Kiera. "But you, ma, I'm about to fill you up with lead."

"Saaleha!" Kiera yelled, making my head snap in her direction. "I'm still your best friend, you can't—"

"Saaleha, watch out!"

BOOM!

To Be Continued....

Made in the USA
Middletown, DE
05 May 2019